# PURRFECT CHARADE

## THE MYSTERIES OF MAX 68

## NIC SAINT

**PURRFECT CHARADE**

**The Mysteries of Max 68**

Copyright © 2023 by Nic Saint

All rights reserved. No part of this book may be reproduced in any form by any electronic or mechanical means including photocopying, recording, or information storage and retrieval without permission in writing from the author.

This is a work of fiction. Names, characters, places, brands, media, and incidents are either the product of the author's imagination or are used fictitiously. The author acknowledges the trademarked status and trademark owners of various products referenced in this work of fiction, which have been used without permission. The publication/use of these trademarks is not authorized, associated with, or sponsored by the trademark owners.

Edited by Chereese Graves

www.nicsaint.com

Give feedback on the book at: info@nicsaint.com

facebook.com/nicsaintauthor
@nicsaintauthor

First Edition

Printed in the U.S.A

# PURRFECT CHARADE

*All Aboard!*

I know I promised never to set foot aboard another cruise ship, but when Marge and Tex decided to celebrate their twenty-fifth wedding anniversary by taking a cruise, and invite the rest of their extended family to join them, we couldn't possibly stay home at some pet hotel. Which is how we found ourselves on board the Ruritania for a ten-day Caribbean cruise.

And I think I may have finally started enjoying myself to some extent, if not a murder had been committed, and Odelia's dad was being fingered by the ship's detective as one of the possible killers. As it was, we soon were roped into the investigation, interviewing suspects, gathering clues and generally traipsing all over the giant cruise liner in search of a killer.

# PROLOGUE

Jack Harper had been lying on his towel, minding his own business, when he was alerted to the presence of an interruption of the peace and quiet of his pool time by droplets of cold water sprinkling on his person. He opened his eyes but could only see that a person or persons unknown were blocking the sun. He tried to shield his eyes to take in this person but found it hard going. Finally, the person spoke, and as his eyes adjusted, he finally saw her steadily, and he saw her whole. She was a woman of considerably handsome aspect, and when she spoke, there was a lilt of something exotic in the way she formed the words.

"You're in my spot, mister," she said. The way she said it suggested that she didn't think it all that important that he move forthwith. More like amusement that he would have the sheer gall to occupy a spot that had clearly been assigned to her.

"I-I'm sorry," said Jack. "I didn't know."

"That's all right. I guess I could just as well take the spot next to you, Mr..."

"Harper," said Jack, mesmerized by the presence of such a gorgeous creature standing a mere foot away from him. "Jack Harper. And you are..."

"Madeline," said the woman, and proceeded to position herself on the sun lounger right next to his.

As they were pretty much the only people present at the pool at this early hour, there were plenty of spaces to choose from, which is why he hadn't really considered that any of these spots would have been reserved. As a cruise ship newbie, he was still trying to come to terms with the ins and outs of cruise ship traveling, and so if he stepped on a few toes from time to time, it wasn't out of malice but simply because he didn't know what the correct etiquette was.

"You a first-time traveler, Jack?" asked Madeline now as she languidly started applying what looked like sunscreen to her bronzed skin. It looked like satin, he decided. And for some reason, he felt a powerful urge to reach out and touch it. But of course, he refrained from doing so. He might be a cruise ship newbie, but at least he knew he shouldn't go about touching completely strange women. That kind of behavior might see him kicked off the boat, and then where would he be?

"Yeah, this is my first time traveling on the Ruritania, actually," he confessed. "Why? Is it that obvious?"

She laughed, a tinkling sort of laugh. "Yeah, pretty much," she said. "But you picked a great one for your first trip, Jack. The Ruritania is probably the best ship traveling the seven seas at the moment. Built in Germany, she's one of the highest quality and largest cruise liners ever built. And it shows."

"You seem to know a lot about cruise liners," he said admiringly. "I take it this isn't your first time traveling on the Ruritania?"

"Oh, no, I've traveled on her loads of times. All the time,

in fact." She gave him a radiant smile that could compete with the sun for first place in sheer radiance. "I live on board, you see. I'm part of the crew."

"Oh, you are? That's so great. So what do you do?" he asked, glad for this opportunity to have a chat with the woman before she turned away and disappeared into her own world, as most of the people on board seemed inclined to do. Since he was traveling alone, he had more or less hoped to strike up friendships with some of his fellow passengers, but so far, that hadn't happened yet, so this opportunity to engage someone in conversation was one he wasn't going to pass by.

"I'm the captain," said the woman simply, causing him to goggle at her to some extent. In his mind, captains were these gray-bearded distinguished older men who stood erect and tall and had a sort of iron grip and a look of steel in their icy blue eyes. But this epitome of loveliness looked probably as far removed from the typical image he had of a captain as he could have imagined.

"Your mouth is hanging open, Jack," said Madeline, looking amused.

"I... I'm sorry," he said. "It's just that... I mean you... I mean to say..."

"You don't think a woman can be the captain of a cruise ship?" she asked sweetly. "Is that it?"

"Oh, no!" he hastened to say. "Of course not. It's just that..." He finally gave up. It was probably obvious that he was both baffled and deeply impressed by this revelation.

"There are lots of women captains now," she said. "So you better get used to the idea, Jack. At least if you plan to become a regular cruise ship traveler. And now if you'll excuse me, I'm going to lie here for ten minutes and work on my tan. As you can imagine, captains of cruise vessels don't get a lot of time off, so I was actually hoping to make the most of my off-time."

And with these words, she closed her eyes, and it was clear that their conversation time had come to an end. At least for now. Jack lay back on his sun lounger, but try as he might, he couldn't quite see himself capable of relaxing after the startling revelation that the most gorgeous creature that he'd ever met—the woman lying right next to him, in fact—was also by way of being in charge of this entire vessel. It certainly put a very interesting spin on things, and as he gave himself up to thought, he wondered if he should have told her about the reason he was on board the Ruritania. If he had, she might not have smiled at him with such radiance or talked to him with such enjoyment.

No, if she really knew what he was doing on board her boat, she probably would have had him arrested on the spot and locked him up below decks in one of the brigs. Then again, nothing ventured, nothing gained, and so he decided to take a leap of faith.

# CHAPTER 1

Vesta Muffin and her friend Scarlett Canyon hurried to their designated spot at the pool. After having spent a couple of days aboard the Ruritania, they were slowly starting to become acquainted with the habits and the mores on board the vessel. For one thing, if you wanted to have a great spot by the pool, you had to hurry and make sure you beat the other passengers to it. And since some of these passengers were perfectly ready, willing, and also able to kick you in the shins if they thought that would suit their purpose, it was paramount to develop a strategy. And so, along with Scarlett, she had devised just such a method of securing the best spot. It was all about the wrists, she knew. You had to race to the sun loungers from the moment the pool deck was being opened for the day, then flick your towel from afar and cause it to land in the right spot. For the moment your towel had landed on the sun lounger, that lounger was officially yours, and nobody could touch it. It took some doing, and she and Scarlett had spent the better part of their second day on board practicing their throwing technique, but now they were experts, and Scarlett was even better at it than Vesta was. She could throw a mean towel from no less than twenty feet away, beating all the other contestants of the daily race and thus securing herself the perfect spot by the main pool.

It was just one of those things that the travel agency hadn't mentioned in the glossy brochures these companies like to publish, extolling the many advantages and virtues of traveling aboard the cruise line's flagship, the Ruritania, but it was one the two friends had learned in record time.

The same thing applied to breakfast, of course. Even though the crew prided itself on making sure that all passengers were always fed and the breakfast buffet was supplied on a continuous basis during official breakfast hours, Vesta had discovered that if you arrived even half an hour late, a lot of the good stuff was gone, and the buffet looked as if a horde of ravenous wild beasts had attacked it and left nothing but crumbs for those who came behind. So it was important that you lined up in front of the restaurant twenty minutes before the doors were officially opened, and used your elbows to muscle to the front of the line and get in there first. She knew what she wanted, and so did Scarlett, and so the moment they burst through those doors, they were already making a beeline for the sushi rolls filled with raw fish and avocado, getting in there before the vultures arrived.

Others might have said it was a stressful way to start the day, but not for Vesta and Scarlett. It was simply part and parcel of traveling with hundreds or possibly even thousands of other passengers on the same boat. And since they were determined to make the most of their time on the ship, the strategy the two friends had devised suited them perfectly. The only thing they hadn't managed yet was to secure themselves a seat at the captain's table. But they had plans in that regard. Big plans, and they were determined to see them through. Before their voyage was over, Vesta and Scarlett would become the captain's new best friends, even if the man didn't know it yet.

Vesta had seen the captain, and she had decided that he was going to become her second husband, or conversely, Scarlett's first. Handsome as could be, with a distinguished white beard and those cool blue eyes that set him apart from all the other males of the species, she knew that wedding bells would ring out in her near future. But since Scarlett had confessed to her that she had also heard those very same wedding bells ring in her ears, Vesta was quite willing to forgo the big prize and become Scarlett's maid of honor if that's how the dice rolled. But until then, it was every woman for herself, and if Scarlett didn't make a move, she most certainly would.

"Oh, isn't he just the most gorgeous man you have ever seen?" she asked now as she smeared a liberal amount of sunscreen on her chest. "He's just so... captainy, isn't he?"

"He is very captainy," said Scarlett. "But something tells me that we're not the only ones in the running for the big prize, honey." She gestured with her head to the captain as he lay next to a woman of bronzed and exotic aspect, who was amiably chatting with the captain. And if Vesta's eyes weren't deceiving her, the captain wasn't fully impervious to the devious vixen's charms either, as he was grinning like a moron while he listened to whatever the woman was pouring into his ear.

Vesta's face clouded. "Treacherous little minx," she muttered under her breath. "You see that all the time, don't you? Women throwing themselves at the captain like that. Making a total fool of themselves." She could have added that she was just such a woman, and in all likelihood, so was Scarlett. But then they had both determined that the captain was theirs for the taking, and so by all rights he shouldn't engage this other woman in conversation and revel in the dubious privilege.

"She's pretty," said Scarlett, and if Vesta wasn't mistaken, there was a touch of jealousy in her voice.

"I guess so," said Vesta reluctantly. "If you like the type."

"The captain certainly likes the type," said Scarlett.

And as they watched on, the conversation between the two seemed to have come to an end, and they both lay back on their respective sun loungers and closed their eyes. Clearly, the captain had decided that enough was enough and had told the woman in no uncertain terms what he thought of passengers becoming entirely too fresh with him.

Vesta relaxed. And as she started thinking up ways and means of approaching the man and snagging his attention, she knew she was in for a tough time since she was obviously facing stiff competition. But she was nothing if not determined and knew that she would come out the victor in this ruthless campaign she was about to engage in. A captain's wife. Now wouldn't that be something? Then she could move out of her daughter's place and travel the seven seas by the side of her handsome captain, being awarded all the perks that probably went with the position. For one thing, she would never have to struggle to get first dibs on a sun lounger in the morning ever again, for the captain's wife probably had her very own lounger reserved especially for her. Maybe even her own private deck with her own private pool. And she would get the best food at the breakfast buffet, the best cabin, and the best service supplied to her free of charge. And as she freely indulged in her daydream of the kind of glorious life she would lead once she became the Ruritania's First Lady, she didn't notice that a hidden hand had snuck up behind her, grabbed the bag she had brought along that contained her wallet and her phone, then retracted again, removing the items and securing them for its own. The same procedure was repeated seconds later with Scarlett's bag and about a dozen other passengers all enjoying those first rays of sun heating up the pool deck. It was a nice haul, and all perpetrated under the nose of the ship's actual captain, who wasn't the gray-haired man who answered to the name Jack Harper but the woman lying next to him.

# CHAPTER 2

Marge wasn't all that keen on the fact that their cruise wasn't going to take them to the one island she had been looking forward to visiting. It had been on the itinerary when they set out on this journey, but apparently something had gone wrong, and now all of a sudden it wasn't on the schedule anymore. It was a small island in the Caribbean, and she had read great things about it, both about the local population's hospitality and friendliness, but also about the springs located in one of the island's spas, which were supposed to possess rejuvenating qualities and be able to cure any diseases you might be suffering from. And since she had been experiencing a slight pain in her right hand lately, she had been hoping that bathing in that healing spring water, which allegedly sprang up straight from the Earth's core, might alleviate the malady she had.

As it was, her husband of twenty-five years, who was a doctor himself, had told her it was all hogwash, and she shouldn't give credence to a bunch of nonsense stories and local hoodoo. Just a way to fleece the tourists, he had said. If she gave into that sort of thing, she was simply perpetuating a myth and allowing these crooks to continue swindling naive people.

Still, when she read on that day's schedule that the trip to the island had been canceled and the boat would steam ahead to their next destination, she felt a distinct pang of regret. The pain in her hand was one thing, but her granddaughter Grace had developed a sort of skin rash lately on her upper back, and she just knew that a dip in that healing spring water would have cleared it right up.

"I don't understand," she told her daughter while the family was enjoying a nice breakfast. "Why did they decide to skip a trip to Marker Island?"

"Probably because King Kong has been spotted," her husband said in a weak attempt at humor.

She made a face at him. "It's not funny, Tex. I was really looking forward to visiting those springs. They're world-famous, and on TripAdvisor there are lots and lots of very positive comments. Hundreds of them, in fact. It would have cleared up Grace's rash."

Odelia gave her a look of commiseration. "Maybe you can ask the captain?" she suggested. "There must be a reason they decided to change the itinerary. Though if you're worried about Grace's rash, don't be. It's practically gone already, with that new cream Dad prescribed."

"They're probably behind schedule," said Chase, Marge's son-in-law. "So they figured they'd better make up for lost time by skipping a destination or two. It happens."

Chase and Odelia were experienced cruise ship travelers, Marge knew. They had done a cruise for their honeymoon, taking along their cats for that occasion, or at least two of them. This time, to celebrate Tex and Marge's twenty-fifth wedding anniversary, the rest of the family had all chipped in and decided to offer the happy couple a Caribbean cruise, something Marge had been dreaming of for years but which had never materialized. But now it was finally happening.

"I'm sure there will be springs on other islands," said Tex now, giving her a rub across the back. "And if you really want to pay a visit to this particular island, we could always come back next year and do it all over again."

She gave him a grateful look. She knew it probably wouldn't happen, but then again, it might. So she decided to put the whole Marker Island business out of her head and focus on the bright side, which was that she was there with her family, and they were having a great time.

"Where is Gran?" asked Odelia now, looking around. "She wasn't in her cabin when I knocked on the door just now to tell her we were heading out."

"She and Scarlett are lounging by the pool," said Tex. "They got up early again so they could get first dibs on the best spots by the pool and also be the first at the breakfast buffet." He shook his head. "They seem to believe that if you're not first to attack the buffet, there will be nothing left."

"Well, it is true that some food items already seem to be finished," said Odelia as she took a bite from her pancake.

"I thought they kept refreshing all morning," said Marge.

"That's the idea," said Tex. "But sometimes they run out of stuff before everyone has had a chance to sample all the items on display, so they simply move some of the other stuff around so it doesn't look obvious things have run out. Which is something Vesta seems to know very well."

Vesta and Scarlett had quickly become experts at this cruise liner thing, and it was obvious that the two older ladies were having a whale of a time. First dibs on the breakfast buffet, first dibs on the best spots by the pool. And their next plan was to get first dibs on a seat at the captain's table for dinner. So far, that particular honor had escaped them, but Marge was convinced it wouldn't be long before they were glued to the captain and wouldn't let go until the man had promised either of the two friends to marry them.

"They certainly have taken to cruise life like a fish to water," said Chase with a grin.

"They've been looking forward to this cruise so much," said Marge. "They've been reading everything they could lay their hands on and watching documentaries, YouTube videos, and movies about cruise life for months now."

"If I didn't know any better," said Tex, "they might even consider becoming fixtures on the Ruritania." A sort of wistful look had come into his eyes, and Marge knew what he was thinking. If he could unload his mother-in-law onto the cruise line company, it would probably be the best day of his life. But since Ma was one of those people who are an acquired taste, Marge didn't think that would happen. They would simply return her to sender as soon as possible.

She glanced around, and when she saw that their four cats were seated next to the table and snacking from their bowls, she relaxed. She hadn't thought they'd be allowed to bring their cats on board. Pet dogs, yes, by all means, but pet cats? She didn't think she had ever heard of people taking a trip aboard a cruise ship with their cats in tow, but the Ruritania was one of the only cruise liners that allowed pets on board, so they had applied for and received permission to do just that, and so now Max, Dooley, Brutus, and Harriet were all aboard, and even though they were still getting used to it, they didn't seem to be overly put out by the sudden shift of environment.

She picked up the remnants of her soft-boiled egg and deposited it onto Max's plate. She watched with interest how he discarded the white and concentrated on the yolk for some reason. He ate it all, then proceeded to start licking himself, blithely ignoring his benefactor, as most cats do.

She shared a look of amusement with her daughter, who had been watching.

Cats. They love you when they need something, then when they get it, they simply ignore you.

Suddenly there was a sort of commotion near the entrance to the restaurant, which was one of many different restaurants on board the gigantic vessel but had quickly become their favorite. When Marge looked up, she saw that her mother and Scarlett were approaching, and they didn't look happy. Both ladies were dressed in their bathing suits, which wasn't allowed in the restaurant, something the hostess at the entrance of the restaurant was pointing out to them. But Ma being Ma, she simply ignored the woman and steamed on the moment she caught sight of her family.

"We've been robbed!" she shouted from thirty yards away. "Someone stole our phones and our wallets!"

"Oh, Christ," said Chase under his breath.

"And we weren't the only ones," Scarlett added. "At least a dozen people lost their personal possessions, some of them their passports and other valuables!"

"And we tried to complain to the captain, but he said he's not the captain at all!" said Ma and seemed even more aggrieved by this betrayal of her confidence than the actual theft of her stuff.

"What do you mean, the captain isn't the captain?" asked Odelia.

"Just what I'm telling you: we told the captain about our stuff being stolen, and the man had the sheer audacity to claim that he wasn't the captain! Probably trying to shirk his duty!"

"You do know that the captain of the Ruritania is a woman, right?" said Odelia.

The look on both Ma and Scarlett's faces was something to behold.

"A woman!" Ma cried, much aggrieved. "But why?!"

"Because women can captain a boat just as well as men can," Odelia pointed out. "So the man you thought was the captain is probably just another passenger, just like us."

"But... but... but..." Ma sputtered, looking like a kid whose candy had been taken away. "But that's not fair!"

"I get first dibs on the passenger," Scarlett said quickly. And when her friend eyed her in abject dismay, she shrugged. "He may not be the captain, but he's still a very handsome man, honey."

Ma threw up her hands. "This cruise is going to hell in a handbasket!" she yelled, and then she pointed a finger at Chase, for some reason. "You have to find our stuff and arrest this thief, Chase."

"Why me?!" Chase cried.

"Because you're a cop, and it's your duty to do... cop stuff."

"I'm on vacation!" said Chase. "And besides, I don't have any jurisdiction here. Go talk to the captain. The actual captain this time, not some passenger who looks like a captain. He'll probably refer you to the ship's security team, and they'll take your statements and catch this thief."

But Ma wasn't so easily appeased. "I don't trust this captain," she said.

"Why?" asked Odelia. "Because she's a woman?"

"Because she's been cheating us! Making us believe this other guy is the captain."

It was the kind of specious logic Marge's mother excelled at. Only this time she was about to be put in her place, Marge saw, for the actual captain had appeared at their table. She was a woman of Marge's age, with red hair tied back in a ponytail and perfectly attired in a captain's uniform. She gave Ma a look of censure. But when she opened her mouth to speak, she was nothing if not perfectly civil and professional. "The deck steward has informed me about the thefts," she told them. "And I want to apologize on behalf of the crew and tell you that we will do everything in our power to make sure it doesn't happen again and that the thief will be apprehended, and your property returned."

"You shouldn't have put this other guy in charge," said Ma.

The captain gave her a look of confusion. "You mean the deck steward?"

"No, the other captain! When we told him what happened, he said he wasn't the captain, and I don't think it's fair."

The captain simply stared at her and gave her a look that Marge had become quite accustomed to over the years. It was the kind of look a lot of people gave Ma Muffin when she was going well. "I don't understand," she finally confessed.

"Don't listen to her," Tex advised since he never did so himself. "She's had a big shock."

The captain's expression instantly morphed into one of compassion. "Of course you have. And like I said, we'll catch the person responsible and return the stolen items as soon as possible. In the meantime, we would like to offer you free drinks for the rest of your trip, and that goes for your entire party." She made a gesture encompassing all those present at the table, and Marge gave the woman a look of approval. Free drinks all around were a nice way to compensate them for the trouble this thief had caused.

But of course, Ma wouldn't have it. "Who cares about free drinks?" she asked. "You should never have allowed this thief to come on board in the first place. So what you're going to do is hire my granddaughter and her husband, and they'll make sure this never happens again."

"I'm sorry, your granddaughter and her husband?" asked the captain.

"They're cops," said Ma proudly. "And they've solved a lot of cases back home. In fact, they never fail at any task they set themselves, so if you add them to your personnel roster, you can be safe in the knowledge that this thief is as good as caught." And when the captain opened her mouth to speak, Ma waved a hand. "You don't have to thank me. It's the least I can do. And now I would like you to introduce Scarlett to your captain who isn't a captain because she's got first dibs, and even though I like the guy myself, Scarlett is my best friend, and if she wants to marry this guy, I'm not going to stand in the way of her future happiness. So lead the way, my dear, and we will follow."

The captain closed her mouth again, and if the dazed look in her eyes was any indication, she was probably already regretting that she had ever welcomed Vesta Muffin aboard the Ruritania in the first place. But then she wasn't the first, and probably wouldn't be the last, to have a feeling of being sandbagged after making Marge's mom's acquaintance. She often had that effect on people.

# CHAPTER 3

Okay, so I know what you're going to say. After our last terrible ordeal aboard a cruise ship, why did we ever agree to board another one of these horrible contraptions? The thing is, if we hadn't come along, we would have had to stay in Hampton Cove without the benefit of our humans' presence. And since the whole family decided to join Marge and Tex on this trip, they would have had to leave us with one of their neighbors or friends, or even one of those pet hotels that are all the rage. And since the last thing I wanted was to spend the next ten days at a pet hotel, no doubt surrounded by the scum of the earth in the form of canines and other pets, we had no other option but to buckle up and join the journey. So far, I hadn't found my sea paws yet, but I was getting there. Who was enjoying the trip even less than I did was Brutus, whose otherwise nice black shiny fur had acquired a distinctly dull look and who looked a little green around the gills.

"I don't like this, Max," he confessed. "I don't like this at all."

"You mean the thefts?" I asked, for we had been following

the back-and-forth between our humans and the captain with keen attention.

"Oh, who cares about the thefts?" he said miserably. "I don't like this trip, I don't like the boat, I don't like anything about it." He sagged to the floor. "I don't understand why you didn't tell me how absolutely terrible being aboard a boat can be."

"You'll get the hang of it soon enough," I told him. Though when he gave me such a pitiful look that my heart bled, I had the impression that maybe he'd never get the hang of it. Maybe he'd be miserable throughout the whole trip and only be happy again once we returned to port and were home safe and sound once more.

"I like it," Harriet announced happily. She had just stowed away a pretty impressive meal and looked as chipper as she had ever looked. "Say, maybe we could ask the captain if she needs another artist for tonight's entertainment. I could sing a couple of songs and become part of the ship's crew."

We had sat through last night's show, and I had to admit that adding Harriet to the program probably would be a major improvement, since even though she's not the world's best singer, she'd do a better job than the scheduled performer. Not that any of the passengers seemed to mind since they all sang along and generally had a ball. Though the copious amounts of alcoholic beverages most of them had imbibed might also have had something to do with that.

"How about you, Dooley?" I asked. "How are you finding this trip?"

"Oh, it's fine," said Dooley.

"Are you sure?" I asked. "You don't sound all that excited to be here."

"No, it's okay," he assured us. "It's just that..." He glanced up at the table where our humans were still partaking of breakfast and were now discussing the recent events surrounding the theft of Gran and Scarlett's wallets and phones. "I don't know if you've noticed, Max, but there's something in the water, and it's been following us all along. I think it probably started following us the moment we left port, and it's been following us ever since."

We all stared at our friend. "What is following us?" asked Brutus, his face turning even paler than before.

"I'm not sure," said Dooley. "Though if I were to hazard a guess, I would say it's probably a giant squid. Or it could be a shoal of sharks, of course, hoping one of the passengers will fall overboard so they can eat them. But like I said, I'm not sure." He shrugged. "I would need to do more research."

I think it's safe to say we all shivered after this shocking announcement from our resident sea expert. In anticipation of this trip, Dooley had watched even more Discovery Channel than usual and had even gone online to brush up on his knowledge of everything to do with taking long journeys aboard a boat. He'd even watched videos of Captain Cousteau, who had been something of a legend in French maritime circles and an avid explorer of sea life. So if Dooley said the boat was being tracked by a large squid or a shoal of sharks, then he probably wasn't too far off the mark.

"But why would a giant squid follow us?" asked Harriet.

Dooley nodded wisely. "For the exact same reason the sharks do. To feed on human flesh. And since people fall overboard all the time, they stand a pretty good chance at being rewarded for their patience." He gave us a serious look. "So whatever you do, don't fall overboard, you guys. You'll be snapped up immediately and become giant squid or shark food. Don't say I didn't warn you."

And with these words, he returned to his breakfast, which today consisted of shrimp. But even though I love shrimp, something we rarely get to feast on at home, somehow I'd lost my appetite. And as I thought about the prospect of being eaten by a giant squid or a shark, I vowed not to set another paw on deck for as long as we were guests on the Ruritania. Best not to take any chances!

Gran and Scarlett had joined our humans at the breakfast table, and as I glanced up, I saw that two more members of our party had decided to participate. They were Uncle Alec and his fiancée Charlene Butterwick. Apparently, they had slept in, and only now were induced by the rumbling sensation in their stomachs to join the rest of the family.

"I was robbed, Alec!" Gran immediately announced, effectively wiping the happy and relaxed smile off her son's face. "Robbed, I tell you. So what are you going to do about it, huh?"

"What are you talking about?" said Uncle Alec as he briefly glanced over to the buffet. Seeing it was still moderately stocked, he relaxed.

"Scarlett and I were at the pool discussing Scarlett's wedding plans when suddenly we both noticed that someone had stolen our wallets and our phones from our bags."

"Tough," was Uncle Alec's only comment. He then excused himself and hurried to pick up a tray and fill it to his heart's content with breakfast items.

"Tough!" said Gran, sounding incredulous. "Is that all he's got to say? First Chase refuses to help us out, and now my own son! What good is it to have cops in the family when they won't even lift a finger to help you when you're being robbed at gunpoint!"

"Gunpoint?" asked Marge, alarmed. "Did the guy have a gun?"

"It's just a matter of speech," Gran clarified, "but it wouldn't surprise me if this miscreant did indeed wield a gun, just in case one of his victims caught sight of him in action and decided to do something about it." She turned to her friend. "Looks like we had a lucky escape, honey. For the same token, he could have shot us both stone-cold dead!"

"I don't think he had a gun," said Scarlett, offering an alternative view. "Guns probably aren't allowed on board. And we did have to pass a guy waving a wand when we boarded, remember?"

"Oh, they've got ways to sneak a gun past the wand," Gran assured her friend. "No, I'm telling you, there's a gang of thieves on board this ship, armed to the teeth, and if we don't do something about it, they'll probably lay waste to the entire group of passengers!"

Charlene, who had joined her future husband to load her tray full of breakfast goodies, now returned, looking fresh as a daisy and with a happy smile on her face. Being away from the office and the business of managing the town of Hampton Cove of which she was the mayor became her.

"This is so nice, you guys," she announced. "Though I'm probably going to gain about ten pounds if I keep this up. This buffet is so amazing, and I just want to keep loading stuff onto my tray!"

"That's both the beauty and the danger of these buffets," said Tex. "Everything is so delicious, you want to try it all, and before you know it, you need two trays to carry everything and two stomachs to digest it all."

"Okay, so I'm going to give myself permission to go all out," said Charlene as she took a seat at the table and eyed her little haul with gratification. "And then once we're back home, I'm going on a diet. How does that sound?"

"Lousy," said Gran. "So are you just going to sit there and stuff your face while Scarlett and I are being robbed of our possessions?"

Charlene frowned. "You guys were robbed?"

"Yes, we were! And at gunpoint, no less!"

"Not at gunpoint," Marge hastened to say.

"But we were robbed," said Gran.

"The captain has promised us she will catch the thief," Odelia told Charlene. "And she's going to return everything that was stolen to the rightful owners."

"I'll believe it when I see it," said Gran, continuing to offer the critical view.

Meanwhile, Uncle Alec had returned, his tray full to overflowing.

"Are you going to eat all of that?" asked Marge with a laugh.

"I'm going to give it my best shot," said Uncle Alec with a happy grin. He then sighed happily. "Now isn't this the life? I could get used to this, you know."

"Yeah, me too," said Chase as he settled back in his chair. His tray was empty, having transferred its contents to his inner trencherman, and he looked ready to take a little siesta by the pool. The only one who didn't look as if she had overdone herself was Grace, but then she only ate what she was being given, and to Odelia's credit, she was limiting the toddler's intake of food to what she needed.

"I like the cruise," Grace now announced. "I like it almost as much as daycare."

"You're a very lucky girl," said Harriet. "To be going on a cruise at your age."

"I just wish there were other kids," Grace said, offering a minor note of critique.

"I'm sure there are lots and lots of kids," I said. "You just haven't met them yet."

Even though the cruise ship offered daycare and even supervised mealtimes for kids who stayed on board during port days, Odelia and Chase had opted to stay with Grace themselves, and to accompany her while she had fun on the waterslides, played in the different pools on offer, and generally had a ball. They were there to have fun as a family, and so the whole family had been joining the activities geared for kids so they could spend this vacation together. The adult contingent, meanwhile, had mainly been relaxing and staying in the vicinity as much as possible, though I have to say that this whole pool aspect didn't sit well with me. Frolicking in a pool isn't my idea of a fun time being had by all. In fact, I couldn't think of anything less fun than being submerged in a very large receptacle filled with water, dozens and dozens of people splashing about, kids sliding down waterslides, and generally getting wet all the time. Brrr.

But then, since I'm not a spoilsport or a wet blanket in any way, I had decided early on not to voice my reservations, and my friends clearly felt the same way, for when Odelia had asked us at the end of our first full day on board the Ruritania if we were having a good time, we had all nodded enthusiastically and said we'd never enjoyed ourselves more. And she actually believed us!

But let's be honest: who in their right mind would voluntarily set foot on board a gigantic floating metal tub and head out in the middle of an entire ocean? You'd have to be crazy to think this constitutes 'fun' in any way. More like suicide, in my personal opinion, or the figments of a deranged mind. But then of course I'm just a cat, so what do I know?

Breakfast over, the human contingent returned to their cabins to get ready for a day of poolside enjoyment, while the four of us dragged our paws to some extent as we patiently waited until our humans were ready so we could spend the day in the shade, a safe distance from the pool, and take long naps while we dreamed of feeling dry land underneath our paws once more.

For the next couple of hours, Marge read her thick tome, which she called a beach read, even though there were no beaches on the ship, Tex simply closed his eyes and promptly fell asleep, Chase and Odelia spent all day in the pool with

Grace, Uncle Alec did his best impression of a beached whale, and Charlene surfed on her phone, a pair of oversized sunglasses on her nose, looking like a movie star of old in her stylish bathing suit. As for Gran and Scarlett, there was no trace of them, so I assumed they were probably on the hunt for the captain who wasn't a captain.

As far as I was concerned, I decided to follow Tex's formula. So I closed my eyes and took a prolonged nap, as did my friends.

Except perhaps Dooley, who kept darting anxious glances to the ship's stern, or is it aft? Presumably on the lookout for that giant squid or that shoal of sharks. If you're the group's designated sea life specialist, you have a responsibility to act as a watchcat, and clearly he took this responsibility very seriously indeed!

And I had just been dreaming of my spot on the couch back home when a sort of roar arose in my vicinity. Immediately, I opened my eyes, fully expecting to see a giant squid tentacle reaching out and picking up people left and right. But instead, all I saw was a very large woman with a very red face looking down at me and shouting something that at first I didn't understand. Finally, I tuned in and heard her say, "Who brought these cats on board! Don't you know I'm allergic?!"

As if people splashing in a pool, giant squids, sharks, and thieves weren't enough to contend with, now we had to deal with a cat hater too!

## CHAPTER 4

Odelia had been playing in the pool with Grace when she became aware of some kind of ruckus taking place nearby. Loud piercing voices penetrated the pleasant wall of noise of playing kids and splashing water near the waterslide that Grace enjoyed so much. When she looked over, she saw her mom and dad had gotten up from their loungers and seemed to be engaged in a heated discussion with a woman of sizable proportions. So she asked her husband to look after their daughter for a moment while she went over there to see what was going on. It didn't take her long to ascertain that the point of contention seemed to be the cats they had brought along with them on the cruise.

"You can't take cats on board. It's against the rules!" the woman was practically screeching at the top of her lungs.

"That's not true," Mom was saying. "Cats are perfectly allowed, just as dogs are allowed, as long as they're not too big and don't cause any trouble. And our cats certainly don't cause trouble for anyone, I can promise you that."

"They're already causing trouble right now!" said the

woman, who seemed to be apoplectic with anger. She pointed at her arm, where a red spot had appeared. "See that? That's because of those cats of yours. And by this time tomorrow, I'll be full of them. And that's because I'm allergic to cats."

"How can anyone be allergic to cats?" asked Uncle Alec with a laugh. "They're not seafood."

The woman gave him a look that could kill. "Well, I am allergic, and if you don't believe me, ask my doctor."

"I'm a doctor, actually," said Odelia's dad, stepping to the fore. "And it's true that cat allergy is all too real. Some people even develop breathing problems within minutes of coming into contact with a cat."

"First time I've heard of such a silly thing," Uncle Alec grumbled.

"If I drop dead right now," said the woman, still speaking in a raised voice, "it's all your fault. And trust me when I tell you that I'll see you all in court!"

Odelia could have told her that she would find it hard to sue them if she was dead, but since she didn't want to pour oil on the flames, she refrained from making the comment. Instead, she said, "We'll put them in our cabins for now. Will that help with your cat allergy?"

The woman glanced over at her and seemed to like what she saw, for she nodded. "I guess so. As long as I don't have to be anywhere near them, I'll be fine. I've got some antihistamines in my cabin. I'll take some, and I hope that will get rid of the itching."

"Best take some eye drops, too," Dad advised as he pointed to the woman's face. "Your eyes are turning red, Mrs..."

"Davis," said the woman, becoming calmer. "Is it bad?"

"I'm sure it'll be all right," said Dad, having adopted his best bedside manner, which never failed to put people at ease. "If you want, I'll accompany you to the medical center to make sure you get the treatment you need."

"Thank you, doctor. I didn't expect there to be cats on board, you see, or otherwise I would have brought a full range of medication."

"I'm sure they'll have what you need at the medical center," said Dad soothingly. And as he led the woman away so they could give her a once-over, he gestured to the cats with his head. His meaning was clear: by the time he and Mrs. Davis returned, those cats better be gone.

And so Odelia took it upon herself to escort her clowder of cats to her cabin, where they wouldn't trigger any other passenger's allergies. Another person approached, a large man this time, and judging from the rash on his arm, he was also suffering from the same malady Mrs. Davis was suffering from.

"Don't tell me," she said as the man stared down at the cats with a curious look on his face. "Also allergic to cats?"

"Oh, no," the man assured her. "I'm a vet, so I'm used to being around cats. I was just wondering... that big orange one, has he had those spots on his nose long?"

Odelia immediately crouched down to study Max's nose. It was just as the man had said: there were indeed a number of spots on his nose she hadn't seen there before. She glanced up at the vet. "What are they?"

The man gave her a look of intense concern, which made her heart sink. "I won't lie to you," he said. "It could be skin cancer. So if I were you, I'd take him to the vet as soon as you return home."

"Could you..." She swallowed away a lump of concern. "Could you take a look at him, please? Make sure he's all right?"

The man gave her a nod. "I'm on vacation right now, so I didn't bring my medical bag. But of course I will take a closer look if you like." He gave her a reassuring smile. "I'm sure it's nothing to worry about, but better to be safe than sorry, right?"

"Absolutely," said Odelia. "Thank you so much. If something were to happen to him, I don't know what I'd do."

"I have an orange kitty at home myself," he said. "So I know exactly how you feel. You can't help but worry over the little fellas."

"Thank you so much," she said, her heart overflowing with gratitude. If Max really had developed some type of skin cancer... Which is why she decided that maybe it was for the best if he didn't venture out of her cabin at all. Being out in the sun all day like this was probably the worst she could have done to him. Poor Max. He was looking at her as if he'd just received a death sentence.

And so she led the vet to her and Chase's cabin, the cats following in their wake. She used her key card to get in, and Max, anticipating what was to come, reluctantly jumped on top of the small table placed near the window and awaited further events. The vet studied his nose up close and finally said with a look of concern, "I would like to keep an eye on him. If the spots become bigger or change color, we probably should start him on a treatment straight away."

"What treatment?" asked Odelia in a tremulous voice.

The doctor grimaced. "The best thing would be to remove the tumor," he told her. "Which means we'd have to operate. And if that's not an option, we have to consider radiation or cryotherapy, which means freezing the cancer cells." When Odelia felt on the verge of tears at these words, the doctor gave her a reassuring look. "In most cases, surgery is the best option. Simply removing the cancerous cells should do the trick. And since they have all the equipment we need at the medical center, if you like I could perform the procedure right there. But only if it's necessary, and if his condition worsens. If not, I'd take him straight to the vet once you get home, and they'll advise you on the correct procedure. Do you have his pet passport, by any chance?"

"Thank you so much," she said, as she took Max's passport from the little wall safe. Gratitude had made her eyes well up. "Max means so much to me, you know. To think I may have caused this cancer by taking him on this trip..."

"Oh, no," the vet assured her as he briefly studied Max's pet passport then handed it back to her. "These spots don't develop over the course of a couple of days. The skin damage was likely caused years ago, and only now has developed into this dangerous growth."

"So... could you keep an eye on him for me? I mean, give him a daily checkup?"

"Absolutely," said the man, then extended his hand. "I don't think we've actually been introduced. My name is Oliver Pearce."

"Odelia Kingsley," she said, "and this is Max."

"Pleased to meet you, Max," said the doctor warmly.

"I wish I could say the same thing," said Max miserably.

She would have told him not to be rude, but since Doctor Pearce couldn't understand what Max was saying, she didn't. Besides, he probably wouldn't have taken well to her starting to communicate with her cat. Most people didn't.

The vet took his leave, and when she turned back, she saw she had a captive audience. All four of her cats were looking at her with anxious expressions on their faces.

"Is Max going to die?" asked Dooley.

"Do I also have spots on my nose?" asked Harriet. "I do, don't I?"

"My spots are probably hidden underneath my fur," Brutus grunted. "Oh, curse this black fur of mine. I may have developed cancer, and I'll be dead before anyone notices."

"Is Max going to die?" Dooley repeated.

"I don't feel any spots," said Max. "Are you sure they're even there?" He had extended his tongue and was trying to trace the outline of the spots.

"Oh, they're there," said Harriet. "Big brown spots." She winced. "Ugly, too. I was going to tell you to get those looked at, but since I knew you wouldn't listen, I didn't. Now of course I wish I had."

"Is Max going to die?" asked Dooley again.

"No, he's not," said Odelia. "The doctor is going to remove those spots, and Max is going to be all right. But I think it's best if you guys stay out of the sun for the time being. It can be very treacherous, as you can see. So I want you to stay here for now. Is that understood?"

They all nodded. "Yes, Odelia," murmured Harriet obediently.

"So... Max is not going to die?" asked Dooley, just to make sure.

"No, Max is not going to die," she said emphatically. Though in all honesty, she knew she wasn't sanguine herself. If those spots became worse, anything could happen. And as she watched those anxious looks on her cats' faces, she thought that maybe she shouldn't tell her mom. After all, they were here to celebrate their twenty-fifth wedding anniversary, not to worry about the fate of their cats. So as she closed the door behind her, she vowed to keep Max's condition a secret for now. She didn't want to spoil the others' vacation. And as she returned to the pool deck, she saw that Dad had also returned and was already lying with his eyes closed and relaxing next to Mom. The latter was reading her beach read, her large-brimmed hat shielding her eyes from the sun. Uncle Alec was splashing in the pool, and so was Charlene, and she joined her husband who was just catching Grace as she zoomed down the chute, laughing all the while.

"So? How bad is it?" asked Chase.

She shook her head. "He doesn't know. I think he probably needs to run some tests. He did tell me that if necessary, he can operate with the equipment they have on board."

"That bad, huh?"

She nodded but then saw that Grace was eyeing her intently, and since she didn't want to alarm her daughter, she forced a smile on her face. "And now we're going to slide down that waterslide together, and Daddy is going to catch us both!" she announced, causing Grace to giggle with anticipatory glee.

## CHAPTER 5

Okay, so most people would consider the verdict Odelia had given us as some kind of punishment. Being locked up in a small on-board cabin and not allowed to venture out? I bet anyone would hate the prospect of having to endure this kind of predicament. But frankly speaking, I didn't mind. As I've already indicated, cats aren't all that fond of pools or oceans or anything to do with either small or large bodies of water. And so, all in all, I was glad that now we had the perfect excuse to stay indoors, lie around, and spend a perfectly lazy time in our room. Though of course the reason for this decision wasn't such a pleasant one at all.

"Cancer, Max!" Dooley cried as he studied my nose up close. "Cancer!"

"I know, Dooley," I told him. "I heard what the vet said, so you don't have to keep repeating it." He was practically glued to my face now, checking out my nose as if it was a bug under a microscope, which maybe to a scientist to some extent it was.

"I knew it," said Brutus, who had adopted a sort of

maudlin mood. "I knew this trip would end in tragedy. Now Max will die, and we'll all be left without our good friend."

"I'm not going to die!" I assured him. "I'm not," I repeated when my three friends looked at me with a sort of sad look on their faces. "For one thing, I'm entirely too young to die. And also, the doctor said that it's absolutely curable. All they have to do is remove the spot, and that's it."

"They'll have to cut your nose open, Max," said Brutus. "Cut it open with a knife!"

I gulped a little. It was another aspect of the matter that did not appeal to me a great deal, I have to admit.

"I'm sure they'll give Max a shot first," said Harriet. "To knock him out. And then they'll cut off his nose."

"They're going to cut off your nose, Max!" Dooley lamented. "You won't have a nose left! And then how are you going to sniff? How are you going to live?"

"I'm sure they won't cut off my nose," I said. "Just a small sliver of skin. The stuff that shouldn't be there."

Dooley had once again resumed his position up close and personal and was now poking at my nose for some reason. "It does look very suspicious," he said. Then he closed his eyes and shook his head in visible dismay. "Now why didn't I say anything? I saw those spots, but I figured they were simply freckles, you know. I even thought to myself it was cute that my best friend was getting freckles on his nose. But now I realize I should have said something!"

"Vena should have seen it," said Brutus. "At our last check-up, she should have said something. And she didn't, which in my book constitutes a blatant case of negligence. I think Odelia should sue. If Max doesn't survive this, she should definitely sue Vena for emotional damages and all of that."

"I'm not going to die!" I assured them once again, though it was starting to become clear to me that I could tell them until I was blue in the face, and they would still remain convinced my final hour had struck. So I decided to give up and take a nap. I hopped onto the bed and was about to put down my head when all of a sudden the door opened noiselessly and Doctor Pearce strode in.

I looked up in alarm. Had he remembered something else about my condition that necessitated an emergency procedure?

Dooley obviously thought the same thing, for he cried, "They're going to operate, Max! They're going to cut off your nose right now!"

Oddly enough, the vet didn't seem all that interested in me, or any of us, really. Instead, he moved straight to the small safe next to the television that was bolted to the wall. Moments later, the safe was open, and he was peering inside. As he extracted a small envelope filled with cash, as well as Odelia and Chase's wallets containing their passports and credit cards, a smile lit up the man's face. And before our very eyes, he transferred the contents of the safe to his pocket, then quickly walked out of the room again, quietly closing the door behind him.

The whole procedure hadn't lasted more than twenty seconds, from the moment the man walked in until the moment he walked out again. In fact, things had happened so fast we didn't realize what was going on until it was too late!

"He took Odelia and Chase's money!" Brutus said.

"I think you're right," I said, shocked by what happened.

"I don't think so," said Dooley. "Odelia probably asked him to pick it up for her so she could pay him for his advice. It's normal procedure, you guys, or did you really think a vet would work for free?"

"But then why did he also take their passports?" asked Brutus. "And their credit cards?"

"Because they need their passports for the operation?" Dooley suggested.

For a moment, we were all quiet. Then Harriet said, "I think we have to consider the possibility that Doctor Pearce is a crook."

She was right. Apparently, the man had gleaned the code of the safe when Odelia took out my pet passport, then returned later on to clean out the contents of the safe. "So... is he a vet or is he a thief?" asked Dooley. "Cause it's entirely possible that he's both. A thieving vet. Or a vetting thief."

"I think he's probably not a vet," Harriet ventured.

"Of course he's not a vet!" said Brutus. "He convinces innocent pet owners that there's something wrong with their pets just because they've got some strange spots on their nose, then manages to talk his way into their cabin, takes a good look at the contents of the safe, and returns later to rob them blind."

"Oh, God," said Harriet. "Wait till we tell Odelia. There will be hell to pay for Doctor Pearce!"

But since Odelia had locked us up in her cabin, there was no way we could reach her and warn her that she was the victim of a very cunning thief.

At least there was one bright spot: if Oliver Pearce was a thief and not a vet, that meant my spots weren't cancerous after all. I think Dooley said it best when he yipped, "Max isn't going to die!"

"No, but Odelia and Chase will be forced to tighten their belt," said Brutus. "Because our humans have officially been burgled, and all of their money has been stolen, and pretty soon now their bank accounts will probably be emptied out as well."

And on that note, we anxiously awaited Odelia's return.

# CHAPTER 6

Henry Morgan had been lounging by the pool when he decided to head inside. It was all fun to get some sun, but too much of a good thing is probably not that good, and besides, he was starting to suffer from a powerful sensation of thirst. As a recovering alcoholic who'd been dry for the past twenty years, thirst was something he'd had to learn to live with. The trip itself had been gifted to him by his two daughters, who were proud that he had celebrated his twentieth year of sobriety. After all, it isn't as easy to stop drinking as most people seem to think. The attraction of the alcohol demon casts a powerful spell on its adherents, and so when Sophie and Bernadette learned that their dad had managed not to touch a single drop in twenty years and had become a better man because of it, and undoubtedly also a better father, they figured their old dad deserved a treat. And so they had regaled him with the tickets to this trip on his fifty-fifth birthday and had sent him off, telling him he should enjoy himself to the fullest.

Twenty minutes later he was sitting at the bar, nursing his apple juice, when a very lovely lady sat down next to him.

She told him her name was Maude Davis, and she was a widow. She used to do this cruise every year with her husband, but since he had died a year ago, she had decided to keep honoring the same tradition, only traveling with his urn instead of the real man. It all seemed a little ghoulish to Henry. But when he told her he was a widower, but that his wife was buried back home in Philadelphia so he couldn't bring her along on this cruise unless he asked the undertaker to dig her up, Maude Davis at first was shocked, but then laughed so loudly that all those present in the bar turned to them, probably wondering what joke he had told her that was so funny.

Frankly, he had told her the little joke in the hopes of getting rid of her, since the last thing he needed was the company of a woman who was in the same position he was. Her reminiscences of her husband would remind him of Lucy, and that could only lead to trouble. But after she had burst into laughter, he figured maybe she wasn't such bad company after all, and before long, they were chatting pleasantly, exchanging stories about their past, and generally getting along like a couple of sailors on shore leave. All in all, the experience wasn't as painful as he had feared. When she ordered a martini on the rocks and asked him what he wanted, he held up his apple juice and asked for the same again. Unfortunately, due to a change in shifts, a new bartender had taken over from the previous one. The man took one look at Henry's apple juice and put down a new drink. It didn't take Henry long to realize it wasn't apple juice but an appletini, but since he felt a little awkward revealing to his new companion that he was, in fact, a recovering alcoholic and so he shouldn't be drinking this appletini, instead he kept his tongue and downed his drink with distinct relish.

After twenty years dry, it felt good to finally taste alcohol again. So after the first appletini, he ordered a second one, then a third, and by the time he sipped from number five, he was feeling so relaxed and happy that he thanked his lucky stars that Sophie and Bernadette had paid for this cruise. And also that he had met Maude Davis, of course, who was really growing on him with every downed appletini. In fact, he liked her so much that at some point he offered that they continue this pleasant binge they were sharing in his cabin. It wasn't night, so he didn't actually use the term nightcap, but nevertheless he made his meaning perfectly clear. She didn't take kindly to the suggestion, though, because after she had stared at him for the space of perhaps half a minute, she slapped him squarely across the cheek, then abruptly slipped off her bar stool and was off.

And since he was feeling a little sad that he'd blown his chances with this lovely woman, he decided to continue his binge. A strange buzzing sound had started up in his ears, and he wondered if it was a fly or a wasp or some other winged creature circling his head. It took him a while to realize it wasn't a fly but something inside his own head that was buzzing. Which is when he remembered that his doctor had told him twenty years ago that he shouldn't drink since his liver was so damaged, even one more drink might be fatal. The buzzing in his ears was indicative of the bad way he was in, and apparently twenty years sober hadn't changed anything in that department.

He didn't mind, and as his heart beat inside of his chest like a jackhammer, and sweat broke out from all pores, he wondered if this was what dying felt like. At least he'd had one final vacation, and he comforted himself with the thought that very soon now, he'd be seeing Lucy again.

DAVID ADAMS DID NOT like his next-door neighbor. The woman was loud, opinionated, and seemed determined to make an absolute nuisance of herself. And what's more, she had a habit of waking him up at all hours of the night by banging on the wallpaper-thin wall that divided his cabin from hers, just when he had finally fallen asleep. He didn't know what her problem was, but obviously she was one of those troubled souls that shouldn't be allowed to go on vacation unsupervised. As it was, he thought that possibly she was suffering from some mental illness that caused her to behave in such an antisocial way. But since he wasn't a specialist himself, he was reluctant to diagnose her with this or that particular affliction. All he knew was that a mental health professional would have had a field day studying her symptoms and reaching a conclusion.

He had returned early from the top deck where he had enjoyed a game of shuffleboard to lie down because he wasn't feeling well. Too much sun, probably. The doctor had told him before he set out on this journey that he should be careful since he had very light skin and fair hair, and as a rule, he didn't take too well to being exposed to the sun for too long. But he'd used plenty of sunblock and had also worn his long-sleeved shirt and his wide-brimmed straw hat. But still, his head was pounding at the temples, and so he returned to his cabin and lay down, hoping it would go away and he wouldn't have to pay a visit to the ship's medical center.

And he'd just laid down his head when Mrs. Davis started pounding that wall again, uttering guttural sounds as she did. "Oh, God," he murmured as he grabbed his earplugs from the nightstand and inserted them into his ears. Good thing earplugs existed, although he could hear her banging and her loud cries even through the earplugs, which made him decide that maybe he should bite the bullet and contact the purser and ask if he could possibly change cabins. He hated making a nuisance of himself like this, but he was a paying customer just like everyone else aboard the Ruritania, and he had every right to enjoy a peaceful and undisturbed night's sleep. And as his eyes closed and he fervently wished that Mrs. Maude Davis would take her lunacy to a shrink and leave her fellow passengers in peace, he wondered if he shouldn't do something about it himself.

# CHAPTER 7

Lucky for us, it didn't take long for Odelia to pay us a visit. I think she was feeling worried about my condition and wanted to make sure that everything was all right and that I hadn't expired while she was away. The moment she walked in, we brought the empty safe to her attention, and as she suppressed some strong oath, she inspected said safe and couldn't escape the sad truth that she had been hoodwinked, cheated, swindled, and generally played for a fool.

"At least now we know that Max isn't dying," Dooley said, offering her the silver lining.

"Our passports are gone, our credit cards, and all of our money," she said, summing things up nicely. "I should have known there was something fishy about a perfect stranger suddenly deciding that not only does one of my cats have skin cancer, but insisting he come back to the cabin to take a closer look. And then asking for Max's passport, that was a nice touch, and I fell for it like a sucker!"

"Anyone would have fallen for it, Odelia," I told her. "He was very convincing as a vet. Even I believed him."

"We all believed him," said Brutus, and wasn't that the truth. The man had presented us with such a perfect display of the perfect vet that we had all fallen for his act, which had given him the opportunity to check out Odelia's cabin, gain access to her safe's code, and then return later to burgle the place. It was definitely a neat set-up, perfectly executed with a certain sense of panache.

"At least we know what he looks like," said Harriet.

"And we've got his name," said Dooley. "Doctor Oliver Pearce."

"I very much doubt that's his real name," said Odelia as she took out her phone to call her husband. "And I also doubt whether we'll even recognize him when we see him. He was probably wearing a disguise. A wig maybe, or a prosthetic nose, or who knows what else."

"I wonder how many people he's pulled this trick on," I said. "Probably a lot since he had a well-oiled routine that we all fell for."

Moments later, Odelia was in communication with her husband, and before long, Chase came hurrying in. When he was apprised of the facts, he also cursed, with even more conviction than his wife. "I knew we shouldn't have used this flimsy safe," he said. "We should have used the safe deposit boxes at Reception."

A knock at the door sounded, and a smallish man walked in with a thin mustache. He introduced himself as Claude Monier, the ship's detective, and before long, Odelia was explaining to him what had happened. The man didn't seem overly surprised. "It's a trick they've used before," he told us. "They target pet owners, since the Ruritania is one of the rare cruise liners that allow pets on board, and then manage to convince them that there's something seriously wrong with their pet, tell them that they're a vet, and follow the owners to their cabins. They glean the code of the safe and then return later when the coast is clear and empty the safe."

"But if you know this person is operating on board the ship," said Chase, "why haven't you caught him yet?"

"Because he's very clever," said the detective. "This man is a professional, operating below the radar. We've tried luring him out by posing as pet owners ourselves, hoping to trap them, but he must possess a sixth sense, for he hasn't fallen for the ruse yet."

"Maybe you should ask my mom," Odelia suggested. "This man probably knows your face and also the faces of your colleagues. But he doesn't know my mother, so you might be able to draw him out that way."

The detective gave her a supercilious little smile. "I'll take it under advisement," he assured her, though it was obvious that working with Odelia or her mother was the last thing on his mind.

"I'm actually a cop myself," Chase said, "Hampton Cove Police Department. So if you need a hand with the investigation, just say the word, and I'm your guy."

"Oh, no, that won't be necessary," said the detective. "I'm sure it's only a matter of time before we catch this person, and then we'll be able to return the stolen goods to their rightful owners."

Odelia stared at the guy. "So this has happened to other people on this voyage?"

The detective nodded reluctantly, the smile never leaving his face, which was disconcerting, for I could tell he wasn't really in a smiling mood. And it wasn't hard to see why. Passengers being robbed probably wasn't part of the fun experience the cruise line company vowed to offer its guests.

"We'll catch this man," he reiterated. "And maybe for now, I would suggest not to befriend any more vets making unbidden diagnoses of your pets." He gave us a look of distinct distaste, indicating that he was certainly not a pet lover himself, and then left the room without giving us much to go on, really. Except that he would catch the culprit and return the stolen property. But he hadn't given us any time frame or even projected any confidence he knew what he was doing.

Which is probably why Chase turned to his wife and said, "Let's catch this guy ourselves, babe."

"Yeah, let's," said Odelia. She then turned to us. "And you're going to help us catch him."

"But what about Max's skin cancer!" Dooley cried before realizing, "Oh, that's right. He doesn't have skin cancer. Just freckles."

"It's because he's getting old," said Brutus with a grin. "Only old cats get freckles. And especially orange ones like Max."

I would have told him I wasn't orange but blorange, but for some strange reason my heart simply wasn't in it. So I decided to drop the matter. It wasn't the hill I was prepared to die on at that moment, not when my humans had just had all of their money, passports and credit cards stolen.

As Chase called his bank and told them to block their cards, it didn't take long before the look on his face told us that the crook had already used the cards. When he hung up, he said, "He maxed out the cards."

"But how? We haven't pulled into port yet," said Odelia.

"No need," said Chase curtly. "He just went on a shopping spree at the Promenade. Clothes, phones, jewelry... You name it, he got it. And all paid by us. The bank has blocked our cards, and they promise that they'll start an investigation."

"So our money?" said Odelia in a small voice.

Chase grimaced. "They couldn't guarantee it, but there's a

good chance that we'll get our money back. They told me to be more careful next time."

"Oh, God," said Odelia. "This is all my fault, isn't it? If I hadn't led that guy into our cabin and opened our safe in front of him, this would never have happened."

Chase wrapped her in his arms. "What's done is done, babe. And you couldn't have known that the guy was a thief. Heck, even I was convinced that he was the real deal. He hit your weak spot—your cats—and then manipulated you into doing what he wanted—opening that safe—by instilling in you a sense of panic and fear and also urgency. I have to say the guy is good. Real good."

"Yeah, he most certainly is," Odelia agreed.

"We'll catch him, won't we, Max?" said Dooley. "We'll catch him and make him pay back all of the money he stole from us."

"We'll catch him," I agreed.

"And then we'll scratch him," Brutus added on a darker note. Clearly seeing our humans upset to such a degree, rankled the big black cat. And I didn't blame him. Stealing people's money and personal property is a vile thing to do. Especially by convincing them their pet has cancer and might die. Personally, I didn't like the man at all. Not one bit. But before we had a chance to agree on a strategy for how to find the thief, there was another knock at the door, and the detective was back.

"Have you found the thief already?" asked Odelia, hope causing her voice to rise in pitch.

But the detective shook his head. He turned to Chase. "Did you say you're a policeman, sir?"

"That's right. Hampton Cove PD, and before that I was with the NYPD."

The man grimaced. "I may need to appeal to your expertise, sir."

"Oh? Is it the thief? Did he strike again?"

"No, I'm afraid there's been an incident." He coughed a delicate cough into his fist, glanced behind him, then lowered his voice. "There's been a, um... Well, there's been a murder."

# CHAPTER 8

*V*esta and Scarlett had gone in search of their 'captain,' but so far, the man had managed to elude them. Of course, there were probably thousands of people on board the Ruritania, so to go through them all would be impossible. They had lounged by the pool where they had first seen the man, then had decided that maybe he would hang out at the spa center. But when that hadn't yielded a hit either, they had headed down to the Promenade, the main shopping lane located at the heart of the ship, to see if they couldn't sniff out the man's trail. And they had just entered their tenth boutique when they hit the jackpot. The captain was trying on a nice pair of board shorts and looking absolutely snazzy as he did.

"Okay, so I know we agreed that you had first dibs on the guy," said Vesta as they watched from behind a male mannequin. "But what if we decide to let him choose?"

"You mean we both introduce ourselves, and if he picks you, I gracefully bow out, and if he goes for me instead, you do the same?"

"Exactly," said Vesta. "I knew you'd understand." She

gave her friend a fervent look. "I like this guy, Scarlett. I really like him. He's got everything I want in a man. He's got a nice beard, great sense of style, he's got a killer smile, and I'm sure that once we get talking, we would hit it off together."

"The same here," said Scarlett, as she eyed the man up and down.

"Okay, so how shall we play this?" asked Vesta.

"We can always pretend to bump into him," Scarlett suggested. "Works every time."

"It's true," Vesta agreed.

And so it was arranged. They would bump into the man and take it from there. They emerged from behind the mannequin and approached the guy. Scarlett got there first, and as she bumped into the man from the right, moments later Vesta bumped into him from the left. The upshot was that the captain went down like a ton of bricks since both women had sped up to reach him first. As he stared up at the duo, a look of surprise on his handsome captainy face, Scarlett was the first to bend over to help him back to his feet. Unfortunately for the guy—or fortunately—Scarlett was dressed in typical fashion with the type of vertiginous décolletage she favored. And as the man got a close-up look at her assets on full display, Vesta could see his eyes practically pop out of his head, his face turn a darker shade of puce, his jaw drop a couple of inches and his beard develop a distinct waggle.

She sighed and knew she had lost the first battle. But then nothing and no one was capable of competing with Scarlett when she decided to throw the full weight of her attributes into play.

The man, finally having been restored to full perpendicularity, his eyes still lost in Scarlett's vertiginous cleavage, was having a hard time keeping his balance. Finally Scarlett cleared her throat and said, "I hope we didn't hurt you, sir. We didn't see you there, did we, Vesta?"

"No, we didn't see you," said Vesta curtly. She held out her hand. "Vesta Muffin, at your service."

"Scarlett Canyon," said Scarlett sweetly. "Also at your service, Mr..."

"Harper," said the guy in a croaky voice. "Jack Harper." Finally, he managed to return his eyes where they were supposed to be, and he grinned. "Nice to make your acquaintance, Mrs. Scarlett."

"Miss Scarlett," she quickly corrected him. "I'm not married."

"Me neither," said Vesta. "I was married once, but the guy died."

"She didn't kill him, if that's what you think," said Scarlett, in what was probably supposed to pass as humor. Vesta didn't think it was funny, though.

"He probably died because you decided to have sex with him in my house, on my kitchen table. His heart couldn't take it, and he croaked."

"He died long after we broke up," Scarlett pointed out. "So you can't put Jack dying on me, honey."

"Oh, your husband's name was also Jack?" asked Jack.

"Yeah, it was," said Vesta. "Strange coincidence, huh?"

"It is a strange coincidence," said Scarlett with a throaty laugh. She had placed her hand on the man's chest and was gazing into his eyes now. "Don't listen to my friend. I never killed anyone in my life."

"You did seduce my husband," Vesta grumbled nastily.

"Or he seduced me," Scarlett said. "Have you ever considered that?"

"Oh, don't give me that crap," said Vesta. "You seduced Jack the same way you seduce any man you meet, by swinging those big—"

"Let's take this somewhere more private, shall we?" Scarlett suggested to the guy as she led him away.

Vesta watched them leave, and she didn't mind admitting that she was quietly fuming. They had a deal. They were going to allow the guy to get to know the two of them and then let him decide. But instead, Scarlett had swept in and was using trickery to seduce the guy and lay claim to him before Vesta even had a chance to get her foot in the door. It was the same thing all over again. Scarlett had seduced Jack back in the day, and she never even had any qualms about it. Well, if she really wanted this fake captain, she was welcome to him. But if things didn't work out, she didn't have to come crying to her. No way!

And deciding that she and Scarlett were friends no more, she stalked off.

\*\*\*

AFTER CHASE HAD LEFT in such a hurry, Marge had been keeping an eye on Grace, and she now wondered what was taking her daughter and Chase so long. "What do you think happened?" she asked her husband.

When Tex didn't respond, she glanced over. As before, her husband was blissfully asleep. The perfect vacation, according to him, was to lounge by the side of the pool, close his eyes, and sleep. And maybe he had a point. He did work very hard back home, seeing to his patients on a daily basis. So he probably deserved a little break.

When Odelia hadn't returned half an hour later, Marge decided to pick up her phone and give her a call. Odelia picked up on the first ring. "There's been a development," her daughter said.

And as she proceeded to fill her in on the theft of their money and credit cards, as well as a murder that had taken place, she placed a hand to her mouth. "Oh no. What are you going to do?"

"I'm not sure," Odelia said. "The ship's detective has asked us to investigate, so naturally we want to lend a helping hand. Do you mind very much, Mom? I mean, I know it's your wedding anniversary, and we're supposed to be spending this time together as a family, so this murder business couldn't have come at a worse time."

"Oh, no, it's fine," she assured her daughter. "You do your thing, honey, and catch this man. Who was it that was murdered? Do you know?"

"Yeah, it's the same woman who was complaining earlier about being allergic to cats, remember?"

"How could I forget? Your dad escorted her to the medical center. Though I'm not sure if they were able to help her." She nudged her husband's shoulder, and immediately he opened his eyes and muttered something unintelligible. When his eyes had finally focused, she asked, "This woman you escorted to the medical center earlier, did they give her something for her allergy?"

"Um... I don't know. I didn't stick around. I simply took her there, then told the doctor what was going on with her and left."

She relayed this information to her daughter and listened for a moment as Odelia assured her they would try to keep the disturbance to a strict minimum. She told her daughter that she was fine with it and that she would continue to babysit Grace for as long as necessary. It wasn't a hardship at all, since she adored her granddaughter. "Do you want me to tell your uncle about this murder?"

"No, don't tell him," said Odelia. "Let him enjoy his vacation."

They disconnected, and as Marge thought about her conversation with Odelia, she wondered how this would impact their vacation. She hoped it wouldn't, for they had enough of these investigations back home. Who would have thought that this type of thing would follow them aboard the Ruritania? But then her daughter seemed to attract this kind of thing. And so did their cats, of course. Which is when she suddenly wondered if the cats would be able to assist Odelia in her investigation. They usually did, but it was different back home. On the ship, it was probably a lot harder to sneak around without being seen. And also, back home they knew every nook and cranny of all the places they were familiar with, while here everything was new and unknown.

Tex's hand stole out and took hers. When she glanced over, she saw he was directing a smile at her.

"What?" she asked.

"Don't worry about it," he said. "You know Odelia. She'll figure it out. Or Max will. Let's just try to relax and have a good time, shall we?"

She nodded. "You're right. But I just can't help—"

"Worrying? There's no need. Everything is fine. Chase and Odelia will catch whoever this person is, and before you know it, things will return to normal again. They always do."

She nodded. "Yeah, I guess you're right." And so she vowed to take both her daughter's and her husband's advice and not let this affect their vacation.

Which is why she was surprised when suddenly a smallish man showed up with a little wisp of a mustache on his upper lip and said, "Tex Poole? Can I please talk to you for a moment, sir? It's in connection to a murder investigation, I'm afraid."

# CHAPTER 9

*E*ven though the ship's detective had decided to enlist Chase's services in catching the person who had committed this murder he had mentioned, that didn't stop him from pursuing his own line of inquiry. We learned this when he suddenly showed up with Tex in tow. Apparently, he seemed to be laboring under the impression that the good doctor was somehow involved in the murder, something Odelia could have easily dissuaded him from. But then Claude Monier struck me as the kind of person who was used to going his own way and not consulting with the person or persons he had asked to give him a hand.

"This is my dad," Odelia pointed out.

"Your dad?" asked the detective.

"Yeah, this is Tex Poole, he's my father."

"Oh," said the detective, and for a moment his eyes crossed back and forth between Odelia and Tex, as if to ascertain whether there was indeed a resemblance or not. Finally, he shrugged. "He's one of the last persons to see Mrs. Davis alive, so I figured I'd ask him a couple of questions."

We were in the detective's office, located not far from the captain's quarters. The office was pretty cramped, especially when it had to fit four adults and four cats. Even though Mr. Monier had expressed a distinct wish not to involve her cats, Odelia had insisted that she couldn't simply leave them behind, and anyway, they weren't going to cause anyone any trouble. And since Claude was clearly in need of a helping hand, he reluctantly allowed Odelia to indulge in her eccentricity.

"Can you tell us what happened, sir?" asked Claude.

Tex looked from the detective to his daughter, who finally nodded. Tex shrugged. "There isn't a lot to tell. Mrs. Davis expressed the sentiment that she was badly affected by my daughter's cats, and that her allergies were flaring up. So I suggested taking her to the medical center to have her checked out. I took her there and left her in the capable care of one of the ship's doctors."

"And then what happened?" asked Claude, who had folded his hands behind his back and was gazing at Tex intently, as if hoping to catch him in an incriminating lie of some kind.

"Nothing," said Tex simply. "I left Mrs. Davis in the care of the doctor, like I said, and returned to the pool deck to rejoin my wife and family."

The man played with his mustache for a moment, twisting its ends Hercule Poirot-style as he nodded in what he clearly hoped was an intelligent way. "I see," he said finally. "And you had never met Mrs. Davis before?"

"I had not," said Tex, starting to get a little antsy.

Suddenly, Claude whirled on him. "You are very nervous, *mon ami*. Why is this so?"

"Because you're making me nervous. The way you look at me, as if I'm some kind of murderer."

"Ah-ha!" Claude shouted as if he had caught Tex in something. "I knew it!"

"What do you know?" asked Tex, looking surprised.

"I make you nervous because you feel guilty. And why would you feel guilty if you hadn't murdered Mrs. Davis!"

"But I didn't!" said Tex. "Like I said, I left her at the medical center, and she was still very much alive. The last thing I saw of her, she was complaining about cats in general, telling the doctor what terrible animals they are as a species and showing him the rash she had developed on her neck."

"So she had developed a rash on her neck, eh?"

"Yes, she had."

"Are you quite sure that rash didn't develop *after* you put your hands around her neck and strangled her?!" He was standing on the tips of his toes now and giving the doctor a menacing look.

"Of course not! That rash developed as a consequence of being in close proximity to the cats," the doctor explained, with remarkable patience, I had to say. If I had been in his shoes, I'd already have laid my paws on Claude's neck and squeezed until he stopped asking me a lot of stupid questions.

"Hmm," said Claude, but he clearly wasn't buying it. Then he turned to Chase and Odelia, who had followed the exchange with rising incredulity, and said, "Do you have any further questions for this suspect?"

"No, we don't," said Chase immediately.

"So be it," said Claude reluctantly and gestured to the door. "You may leave, sir, but don't disembark the boat, please. I may have further questions for you at a later date."

"I'm not going to disembark the boat," said Tex. "Because my wife is on the boat, and so is the rest of our family. It's our twenty-fifth wedding anniversary, you see, and we're celebrating it by taking a cruise together. As a family," he stressed.

But the detective was impervious to this appeal to his common sense or his better nature or both. "Don't leave the boat," he barked. And then: "Dismissed!"

After the door had closed, for a few moments a stunned silence hung in the room. Then finally Claude said, "You are probably wondering why I was so hard on your father, Mrs. Kingsley?"

"The thought had crossed my mind," Odelia admitted, not looking very happy.

"I believe in treating every suspect equally," Claude explained as he took a seat behind his desk and steepled his fingers. "I don't play favorites, not even when it concerns relatives of the detective assisting me in a case. Even if my own mother were a suspect, I'd also have interrogated her in the same manner."

"Poor mother," Dooley remarked, and I think he spoke for all of us.

This first interview at an end, Claude seemed to think it judicious to take us to the scene of the crime, something he probably should have done before hauling Tex into his office for this impromptu interrogation. But as he explained to Odelia and Chase, he had a hunch about Tex and felt it was more important to follow his hunch "before the killer could jump ship and abscond."

If Odelia was insulted by this slur on her dad's character, she didn't show it. But then she had switched into professional mode and seemed determined not to let this strange little man's behavior affect her too much. Besides, it wouldn't do her a lot of good if she got on his bad side. He would probably exclude her and Chase from the investigation and arrest Tex. And then where would we be?

We arrived at the cabin where the tragedy had taken place, and as Claude opened the door with his key card, he showed us in, then immediately closed the door again behind us, presumably so no lookie-loos could take a gander at the unfortunate victim of the heinous crime. Before us, stretched out on the bed, lay the body of the woman who had accused us of trying to kill her by triggering her allergies. Somehow, I feared that Claude might arrest us later. But since apparently the woman had been strangled, maybe he wouldn't.

"See?" said Claude as he walked up to the body and pointed at the woman's neck with a pen he had taken from his pocket. "Clearly strangulation marks. Whoever murdered this poor woman must have used a lot of strength."

"He used a piece of rope or some other object," Chase pointed out. "If the killer had used his bare hands, we would see the outline of the separate digits on her neck. But since we only see the ligature marks, it's obvious that the killer used either a piece of rope or some other ligature."

"Of course," said Claude with an indulgent smile. "I was merely testing you, my young friend. No, obviously she was murdered with a rope or, as the case may be, a rope-like object." He pointed to a pair of nylon pantyhose lying next to the bed. He picked it up. "Something like this would make for a good murder weapon." He took it in both hands and yanked it taut. "See? If applied like this, you can use a lot of strength."

"I think that probably is the murder weapon," said Chase dryly.

Immediately, the detective dropped the pantyhose onto the bed as if stung.

"Of course," he muttered. "That would make sense. Strangled with her own pantyhose. This murderer... he is a maniac! He is a psychopath, obsessed with the poor woman's clothes. Maybe he's obsessed with her. He wants to possess her, to own her. She rejects him, so he overpowers her and kills the object of his affection. Basic Freud." He smiled at his counterparts, putting his hands behind his back as he rocked back on the balls of his feet. "I think I've just solved the murder by using simple psychology. We are looking for a man with considerable strength in his hands and forearms. A man who had recently made Mrs. Davis's acquaintance and who had fallen under her spell. He wanted her. He was crazy about her! But when she rejected him, he couldn't take the rejection, and so he pounced!" At these words, he suddenly jumped forward, scaring us all out of our wits. He gave us a reassuring smile. "The murderer was here," he assured us. He stuck his nose in the air and sniffed noisily. "I can smell him." He closed his eyes. "I can see him. I can feel him!"

And before we could stop him, he stalked out of the room and was gone.

"Where... where did he go, Max?" asked Dooley.

"I'm not sure," I confessed.

"Maybe he's got a lead on the killer?" Brutus suggested.

"That man is scary," said Harriet with a shiver. "It wouldn't surprise me if he's the killer."

Chase and Odelia, who looked secretly relieved that Claude had left the room, now examined the victim, Mrs. Davis. Since we had seen her last, she had developed a serious rash on her cheeks, which extended all the way to her ears. I almost didn't recognize her, as her face was swollen, though that could be from the strangulation. But clearly, she hadn't been kidding about her allergy. The rash wasn't what killed her, though. The murderer did. Chase picked up the pantyhose with a pen and studied them closely. "Too bad we don't have access to a team of forensic experts," he said. "Maybe they could have extracted some of the killer's DNA from the murder weapon."

"I doubt it," said Odelia. "If the killer was smart, he would have worn gloves when he killed her."

Chase rifled through the different drawers of a small desk in the corner of the cabin. I saw that, contrary to Claude, he and Odelia were wearing plastic gloves, like the professionals that they were.

"Maude Davis," said Chase as he studied the woman's driver's license. "Los Angeles address."

Odelia had found a phone and tried different combinations before hitting on the right one to unlock it. "One, two, three, four," she murmured as she quickly checked messages, call history, and Mrs. Davis's emails. "This is interesting," she announced as she expertly flicked through the different apps on the phone. "She kept a sort of diary. Wrote notes to herself. Last entry..." She frowned at the display. "'Met a very annoying man at the bar. At first, he seemed nice enough. Widowed, just like me. But the more he drank, the more obnoxious he became. Finally, I had to leave as he started making lewd suggestions.'" She looked up. "Entry made this afternoon at one-thirty."

Chase nodded. "We better have a talk with the bartender to see who this lewd man is. If he didn't take no for an answer, he might have followed Mrs. Davis and killed her in a fit of rage. Especially if he was drunk, as this diary entry seems to indicate."

"So she was a widow," said Odelia. "But that doesn't necessarily mean she was traveling alone." She looked around, then checked the woman's closet. "She certainly didn't share this room with anyone, though. I don't see any evidence that there was a second person staying with her."

"No, and Claude already checked and told us that she checked in by herself," Chase pointed out.

Suddenly, a knock sounded at the door and Claude burst

back in. He looked excited, his green eyes shining with a strange light. "I have made an arrest!" he announced.

"You can't make an arrest," Chase pointed out. "Since you're not a cop."

"No matter," said Claude, making an irritated gesture. "I have a man in custody, and I'm one hundred percent convinced he is our deviant killer!"

# CHAPTER 10

Not all that far from where these tragic events had been taking place, Henry Morgan was sleeping off his bender. When he woke up, his head was hurting like crazy, and immediately the recollection of the events that had led to his falling off the wagon came back to him. As he groaned, both in agony of his painfully throbbing head as well as the realization that he'd broken a dry spell of no less than twenty years, and all because he wanted to make a good impression on some woman he had never met before, he cursed himself and the woman both. Though, of course, it hadn't been her fault, it was his and his alone. Still, she didn't have to be so harsh on him, rejecting him out of hand when he made that suggestion. Unfortunately, after she had left, he had kept on drinking, and as his memory of what had happened was a little fuzzy, he now wondered how he had managed to get into bed in the first place. He certainly didn't remember taking off his shoes or lying down.

Maybe that bartender had shown his humanity and had escorted him out of the bar and then to his room? Try as he might, he simply couldn't remember a single thing. He did remember some kind of altercation, though, as if he'd gotten into a fight with someone. And as he became aware that his hand was hurting, he held it up to his face and scrutinized it. There was a cut on his hand that must have bled, for there was still dried blood in the wound.

It all reminded him of times past when he would wake up after a bender and suffer from a blackout. Back then, he had sworn that it would never happen again, but now it had. So he sighed, took out his phone, and called his accountability partner. He probably should have called him sooner, but then he'd been too busy trying to get in good with this Mrs. Davis he met at the bar.

Joe Wilson picked up on the first ring. "Trouble in paradise?" he asked.

"Yeah, I'm afraid I'm starting from zero again," he said.

"That's all right," said Joe. "You have to start somewhere." He paused. "What happened?"

And so he explained to his good friend how he had more or less been tricked into drinking again. Though, as Joe indicated, he had only managed to trick himself. He could have put down that drink the moment he realized it wasn't apple juice but something a lot stronger and told the bartender that he had given him the wrong order. Or he could have told the woman that he was suffering from an allergy to alcohol and his doctor had told him he shouldn't drink.

"I know you're right," he told the man he'd known for twenty years now. They'd met at his very first AA meeting and had become friends and stayed that way ever since. Joe was thirty years sober and was not just Henry's accountability partner but also a sponsor for a lot of the younger members. He had a fatherly quality that appealed to a lot of people who needed a helping hand and listening ear when things got tough. Henry hadn't needed him for a long time, but today he definitely did.

"Just go easy on yourself," Joe advised. "Don't blame yourself. These things happen, as we all know, so just get yourself up and dust yourself off. No harm done, and get back on the wagon."

"Thanks, Joe," he said, and he meant it.

"No problem. Hey, you should have taken me on that cruise with you, just like you promised. Then this wouldn't have happened."

He grinned. "Yeah, right. Tell Sophie and Bernadette. They're the ones paying for the ticket."

"You're not going to tell them you fell off the wagon the moment you got on board, right?"

He hesitated. "What do you think? Should I tell them?"

"I don't think you should."

"The whole purpose of this trip is to celebrate the fact that I'm twenty years sober this year."

"Yeah, don't tell them."

"I have to, Joe. Otherwise, in five years, they'll think I'm twenty-five years sober, and they'll pay for another trip. I can't lie to them." He had raised his daughters to be honest with him and Lucy, and he had always vowed he would return the favor by being honest with them. He couldn't start lying to them now.

"Okay, so tell them when you get back, not now. You're vulnerable out there on your own, buddy. In a strange environment and surrounded by plenty of temptation."

"I know," he said.

"So just take it easy, don't go near that bar again, and when you feel tempted, just call me, all right?"

"I promise," he said.

They rang off, and he thought he'd better take a pill for that horrible headache of his. He hadn't felt this way in a very long time, and even though he knew he could vow never to touch a drop of alcohol ever again, the mind was a treacherous thing, and so was his addiction. So instead, he told himself he wouldn't touch a drop of alcohol today. And since tomorrow was another day, he'd see what happened. But this advice Joe had given him about not going anywhere near that bar again was golden. Temptation was indeed everywhere, and since he was in a vulnerable state right now, after his recent relapse, it wasn't going to be easy to stay sober throughout the entire trip.

But he was certainly going to give it his best shot.

He also hoped to bump into Maude Davis again so he could apologize for his behavior, which he knew must have been pretty horrible. God knows what she must think of him. Probably that he was a terrible human being for hitting on her like that. And a woman carrying the urn with her husband's ashes on board. What was he thinking?

IT DIDN'T TAKE us long to reach Claude's office again. But instead of going in, the ship's detective walked straight past his office and kept going. At the end of the corridor, he stopped and took out a key to open a door. Setting foot inside, we discovered it was a sort of jail cell, though instead of a jail, he called it the ship's 'brig.' In this brig, seated on a cot, was a man I'd never seen before.

"Without a doubt," said Claude as he stepped aside so we could get a good look at the man, "this is Maude Davis's killer."

"I didn't do it," said the man immediately.

"Shut up," said Claude. "I've got you on CCTV breaking into Mrs. Davis's room, so there's no question that I've got you dead to rights, Mr. Adams."

"Okay, so I went in there," said the guy. "But I didn't kill her. When I entered her room..."

"Yes?" said Chase encouragingly.

"She was already dead. Which is why I immediately left again."

"Why didn't you inform the security team?" asked Odelia.

"Because of this, all right," he said, gesturing to the three people standing in front of him. "I knew you'd try to pin this on me. So I decided not to say anything and let you figure it out."

"Why did you go into Mrs. Davis's cabin?" asked Chase.

The guy sighed and dragged a weary hand through his curly mop of hair. "Because I was trying to take a nap, and she was making so much noise I couldn't sleep. She always did this, even at night she would pound the walls and make it almost impossible for me to fall asleep. I've been thinking for a while to inform the purser and ask for a different room. But this time I was so fed up, I decided to tell her she couldn't keep behaving like this. Even with earplugs I couldn't fall asleep. Only by the time I finally worked up the courage to confront her, the noise had stopped, and the door was ajar. So I pushed it open, and that's when I saw her lying on the bed. I only needed one look to know that she was dead. So I quickly snuck out again and closed the door."

"You should have told me," Claude insisted. "And the fact that you didn't, tells me your story is a lie, Mr. Adams. You were angry with your neighbor. In fact, you were so angry with her for making it impossible for you to go to sleep that you barged into her room and got involved in an argument with her. You lost your temper, and you strangled her. Then you came to your senses, and you quickly left again, forgetting that we have cameras in all the public areas on all the different decks of the ship. And I clearly saw you enter your neighbor's room and quickly sneak out again."

"Look, I know how this looks, but I promise you I didn't kill her, all right?" said the man.

"I'll just leave you here to cool off a little," said Claude. "Because I can see that you're still very aggressive, and I wouldn't want you to attack anyone else. Me, for instance, or my two colleagues."

"Or us," Brutus grunted.

"I don't think this guy is in the habit of attacking cats," Harriet said. "He looks like the harmless sort."

"He does look harmless, doesn't he?" I said. Mr. Adams was a young man with a big crop of curly brown hair and glasses and looked more like an artist than a vicious killer. Though if Mrs. Davis kept him up at night by pounding on the wall all the time, I could imagine that would have made him mad. But did it make him mad enough to kill? It was possible, of course.

Behind us, a door opened, and the captain appeared. She gave us a smile and then addressed Claude. "Have you locked the suspect in the brig, Claude?"

"I did, captain," said Claude dutifully. "I'm convinced he's our man."

"Why didn't you lock him up sooner?"

"Because I belatedly realized that we have CCTV in that corridor, captain. But when I watched the CCTV, I could clearly see David Adams sneak out of his own room, then into Maude Davis's room. Of course, we can't see what happened there, but I think it's obvious. He got so upset over the incessant noise that he lost his head and murdered her in a fit of rage. He fits the profile too."

"He does? In what way?"

"He's an artist, captain," said Claude. "A folk singer. And we all know what artists are like. They lack the kind of self-restraint and the inhibitions normal people naturally possess in spades."

The captain's lips twitched into a tiny smile, and I got the impression that she wasn't fully on board with this novel theory. She now turned to Odelia and Chase. "We weren't properly introduced this morning. I'm Captain Murray. Madeline Murray. And you are Chase and Odelia Kingsley?"

"They're the cops I told you about," Claude reminded her. "Though we won't be needing you anymore now that I got the killer," he added to the couple.

"Let's not jump to conclusions," the captain suggested. "Can I see the CCTV, Claude? Can you show us?"

"Of course," said Claude, and led us to a different office than his own. Here we found, to our surprise, a small team intently watching a bank of screens that showed pretty much every part of the ship.

"This is the security team that runs security aboard the Ruritania," the captain explained. "On a big vessel like this, we need to make sure the safety and security of the passengers is guaranteed at all times. Something we take very seriously indeed." She instructed a member of the security personnel to run the CCTV of the corridor where Maude Davis's cabin was located.

The man had the footage ready, presumably since Claude had asked him the same thing before. As we could clearly see, David Adams left his own room and entered his neighbor's cabin at precisely two minutes past two. He came out again mere seconds later, looking greatly disturbed, hesitated for a moment, then closed the door to Mrs. Davis's cabin and returned to his own.

"See?" said Claude triumphantly. "He's our man, all right."

"He was only in there for ten seconds," Odelia pointed out. "I very much doubt whether he'd have been able to murder Mrs. Davis in that timespan."

"Exactly what I was thinking," said the captain. "Ten seconds isn't long enough to murder a person by strangulation. Am I correct in assuming this, Detective Kingsley?"

Chase shook his head. "It takes minutes to die from strangulation, not seconds. So if this timestamp is correct, David Adams is not our killer."

"But... but he has to be!" said Claude. "It's obvious from the footage!"

"Can you go back ten minutes, Clive?" asked the captain.

"Ten minutes before this moment?" asked the security man.

"Yes, go back ten minutes and let's see if anyone else went into that cabin."

He adjusted some of the settings, and the screen flickered to life again with an image of the corridor. Since we knew where Mrs. Davis's door was, we focused our attention there. It took a while, but suddenly a dark figure appeared, tracked down the corridor, and entered the room of the victim. This time it took longer than ten seconds for the figure to reemerge. At least five minutes passed before the person came out again. As they did, they kept their head down, so the camera didn't pick up their features. And as they disappeared from view again, try as we might, it was impossible even to determine whether it was a man or a woman.

"That is our killer," said Chase, pointing at the screen.

The captain sighed and turned to Claude. "Release Mr. Adams from the brig, Claude."

"But..."

"Let him go. Now."

And so Claude did as he was told. He didn't look happy about it, though.

"Can't you, you know, track the person?" asked Chase as he bent over the guy handling the controls. "Along the corridor and then pick him up with a different camera?"

"Good idea, detective," said the captain. "Do it, Clive."

Clive fiddled with the controls, and moments later, he had caught our killer again, only this time on a different camera. According to the timestamp, only thirty seconds had passed. And as he tracked the killer's progress, we saw how the person reached the Promenade, the main thoroughfare where all the shops are located. The killer now entered one of the boutiques where clothes were sold. But when Clive tried to switch to the camera that monitored the store, he got an error.

"Darn it," he muttered.

"What is it?"

"Looks like the camera is on the fritz again."

"No worries," said Chase. "All we have to do is see who walks out of the store again. Unless there's another exit?"

"Well, there is an exit at the back," said the captain. "All the stores have an emergency exit that leads to a corridor that runs behind the stores." She looked at Clive for his input.

"No cameras there, I'm afraid," the man said. "But chances are that the killer has no idea that this exit is even there. It's hidden behind the fitting rooms."

As we watched on, suddenly Odelia pointed to the screen. "Look, Chase."

"Oh, God," said Chase.

Before our very eyes, Gran and Scarlett had walked into the store and disappeared inside. And as Clive sped up the footage, then stopped each time a person exited the store and made sure to get a close-up and a screenshot, we saw how Scarlett walked back out of the store accompanied by a handsome man with a fashionable beard who clearly couldn't keep his eyes off her. One minute later, Gran followed, and her face spelled storm. Whatever had happened inside the boutique, Gran clearly wasn't happy about it, and it wasn't hard to figure out what had made her that way.

"Too bad we don't have eyes in the store," said Chase. "How long has this camera been broken?"

"A couple of days," said Clive. "We keep fixing it, but it keeps breaking down."

"Is it the camera itself or the circuitry?" When Clive frowned, he explained himself. "This killer clearly knew where all the cameras are located because we never saw his or her face. So what if they scoped out their escape route before the murder and also made sure that the camera in the store was broken because they made it that way? It wouldn't be hard to yank out a wire or something."

"Which is exactly what happened," Clive confirmed. "I figured it was either vandals or the store clerk not wanting to be filmed during working hours. Some people are like that, you know. They hate knowing they're being watched, even though the camera is there for their own safety."

"It makes sense that the killer would be the one who sabotaged the camera," said the captain, nodding. "Good thinking, detective. That means we're looking for a person who was in that store at some point before today, making sure that camera was out of order." She frowned. "Would it be feasible to track every person who went in and out of that store since we left port?"

Clive shook his head. "There must be hundreds of people. Bella Bello is a very popular store. Possibly the most popular one on the whole Promenade."

"Which would make sense," said Odelia. "If the killer knew that, they would have picked it, knowing how difficult it would be for us to discover their identity."

"It's not impossible," said Chase. "We would need to track every single person who walked into that store over the course of the past few days and then compare it to anyone walking out of the store from now until... closing time, I guess."

"We could call the store clerk," Clive suggested, "and ask them if anyone hung around longer than strictly necessary. If not, whoever walked in must have walked out within the next twenty minutes or so, which would follow the normal pattern."

"Unless they knew the exit at the back," Odelia pointed out. "And if this person knew where all the cameras are and made sure to sabotage the camera in the store, it's not unlikely that they were also aware of the back exit and the fact that it isn't covered by any cameras."

A collective sigh descended upon the small company. Clearly, whoever had murdered Mrs. Davis had worked hard on a fool-proof plan of escape. What Odelia said made a lot of sense. Why walk back out of the store and have your face captured by a camera if you can walk out the back unseen?

"I think it's safe to say we've lost our killer already," said the captain, voicing the general opinion of those gathered around that screen.

"Unless..." said Odelia. "The store clerk saw the person entering and remembered them."

"You better head down there and ask," the captain suggested. "Before she can forget."

Chase looked surprised. "You mean..."

The captain nodded. "I know this is unusual, but would you mind terribly taking over the investigation, Detective Kingsley? You're an experienced detective, and frankly speaking, Claude isn't. To be honest, we're not equipped to deal with a murder inquiry. Mostly, we handle thefts, vandalism, public drunkenness, the occasional sexual harassment complaint, but not murder. The cruise line would compensate you for your time, of course, and we would comp your trip."

"Could you also comp my family's trip?" asked Chase.

The captain smiled. "Of course. Consider it done."

"I'll do it," said Chase. "But only if my wife can join me."

"Whatever you need. We have a killer on the loose, and I

won't sleep easy until I know he's been caught and thrown in the brig."

"You've got a deal," said Chase and shook the captain's hand.

Odelia glanced down at us, and I knew just what that look meant.

"Uh-oh," said Harriet. "Looks like we've got a job to do, you guys."

# CHAPTER 11

While Chase and Odelia had access to the captain and the security team, they decided to broach a subject that had been vexing them before this whole murder business had begun, namely the break-in into their cabin and the theft of Gran and Scarlett's wallets and phones on the pool deck.

"You have cameras all over the ship, right?" said Odelia. "So maybe you can find out who burgled our safe and who robbed my grandmother and her friend?"

"No problem," said the captain as she gave a sign to Clive to get on it. "Did you report this?"

"We did," said Chase. "But so far, we haven't heard back."

"It's very unfortunate," said the captain. "But since we run a pretty big ship with about four thousand passengers on board, there are bound to be a few less-than-honest people among them who think this is the perfect opportunity to rob their fellow passengers. We try to keep everybody safe, but it's not always possible to stop these people from boarding the vessel."

Chase had fed Clive the information, and the security

man was busily scanning the footage taken around the time our cabin had been broken into. It didn't take him long to find it. And when he did, the captain grunted in dismay. "I think I know this fellow. He's been the scourge of every ship in our cruise line company. Keeps coming up with fresh angles to target people and eludes capture at every turn. He's a master of disguise, you see, and every time we think we've got him, he manages to get away." She turned to us. "I hope your cats weren't too traumatized by the whole ordeal? They were in the cabin, I presume?"

"Yeah, they were inside and saw—or must have seen—the whole thing," said Odelia. "But I don't think they were harmed in any way."

"Oh, no, he's very careful about not using violence, which, at least, is something good."

"He introduced himself as a vet," said Odelia. "And said he was going to operate on Max, claiming he had a cancerous growth on his nose. But in the end, it was just a ruse to get inside the cabin and learn the combination of the safe."

The captain was nodding. "He always does this. The cruise line has a name for him, you know. We call him Captain Invisible since he seems to be able to disappear into thin air every time we think we're close to capturing him. He's been the bane of our existence for years now. And he doesn't steal a lot. Just targets a couple of people on each trip, not a whole lot. In that sense, he's like a mosquito. His stings hurt, and they're annoying, but he doesn't overdo it and kill the host."

"And what about my grandmother?" asked Odelia as she watched over Clive's shoulder. He was showing the footage from the pool, and even though the camera caught the actual moment their bags were rifled through, it was very subtle. As he zoomed in, all you could see was a hand sneaking into Gran's bag and then retracting again. But since the person the hand belonged to was out of the line of sight of the camera, it was impossible to see his face. I had a sneaking suspicion, though, that it might be Captain Invisible again, only using a different guise this time. The captain seemed to be of the same opinion.

"He knows where all the cameras are," she explained, "and knows how to stay out of sight."

"Do you think he might be responsible for the Maude Davis murder?" asked Chase. "Perhaps he broke into her room thinking she was out and Mrs. Davis caught him burgling her safe, and he killed her because she saw his face?"

"It's possible," the captain allowed. "But highly unlikely. In all the years Captain Invisible has been active, he's never once resorted to violence. It's just not his jam." She gave us a smile. "Our insurance company will compensate you for your loss, of course. Just fill out the necessary paperwork, and I will personally make it happen."

"Thanks," said Odelia warmly. "It's not a lot of fun to go on a trip and then get robbed of your credit cards and all of your money."

"I know, it's a terrible nuisance," the captain concurred. "People take a cruise to have fun and enjoy their time away from the stresses of everyday life. And then when someone like Captain Invisible shows up and robs you blind, it's extremely infuriating."

Clive had been scanning the security footage some more, but as apparently had happened before, it was impossible to get a glimpse of the thief's face. Except when he'd shown his face to Odelia and us, of course, but the captain assured us that when we saw him next, we probably wouldn't recognize him. He certainly wouldn't look like the friendly and helpful vet we had met.

"Imagine being treated for a cancerous growth by a crook," said Brutus.

"He might have stolen that cancerous growth on Max's nose," said Dooley.

"Yeah, if all doctors were as skilled at removing personal items from people's possessions," said Harriet, "the world would probably be rid of all diseases."

Unfortunately, what Captain Invisible stole wasn't suspicious spots on people's noses or other ailments. Instead, he reached deep and took their money, their wallets, their ID cards, and the like. And especially when you were traveling, that created a lot of inconvenience and annoyance.

Now that we had received our marching orders, we said goodbye to the captain and went on our way. We had a murderer to catch and also a burglarious individual who had targeted no less than three members of our extended family. Time to get cracking!

The first person Odelia and Chase chose to talk to was the woman running Bella Bello, the boutique where Mrs. Davis's murderer was seen entering and then mysteriously disappearing again, possibly via the back exit.

Laura Rogers ran the boutique and seemed surprised to see us. But when Odelia explained to her the purpose of our visit, she was very helpful. She was a middle-aged woman with suspiciously blond hair and a serious expression on her face, and when she heard about what happened, she was thoroughly shocked.

"A murder!" she said, bringing a perfectly manicured hand to her face. "But who would do such a thing on a cruise!"

"As if murders didn't happen on cruises," Brutus murmured.

"I guess murders happen everywhere, right?" said Dooley. "Even on cruises?"

"Murders can and do happen everywhere," I agreed. "Though I guess it shocks people more when they hear it's happened while they're on holiday. Just like with the burglaries, you don't expect that kind of thing to happen when you're on vacation."

"No, vacation is about having a fun relaxing time, not having to deal with the darker aspects of life," Harriet said. "Like thieves and murderers."

"I can't say I paid a lot of attention to who entered and left the store," Mrs. Rogers said as she threw her mind back. "I know it was very busy at one point, but then it usually is at this time. We're one of the more popular stores along the Promenade, you see, and so it's not unheard of that we have dozens of shoppers browsing the store, and it was exactly that way this afternoon. When did this... murderer visit the store, you say?"

"At two-twenty," said Odelia. She had taken out the printout Clive had made of the moment the killer had walked into the store, taken from the CCTV which covered the entrance, and showed it to Mrs. Rogers.

"You can't see his face," she said as she studied the picture. "You can't even see if it's a man or a woman. Though if he killed that poor woman, it's probably a man. Murderers are mostly men. Statistically speaking, that is." She gave us an apologetic smile. "I read a lot of true crime books, and that seems to be the case."

"Yeah, I guess that's probably true," Chase allowed, "though I wouldn't discount the possibility that the killer could also be a woman. So you don't remember a person of this description walking into your store at two-twenty?"

Laura shook her head. "I'm sorry, but like I said, it was very busy around that time, and since my colleague called in sick this morning, I've been all over the place. If I had eight arms, it still wouldn't have been enough. So I didn't really pay attention to the entrance, just to the people in the store."

"Don't you have security at the store?" asked Chase.

She nodded. "Normally we do, but Norman was called away. A fight had broken out at the Galleria, two doors down from us, and apparently their security couldn't handle it by themselves so they had called in his assistance. This was shortly after lunch, and I haven't seen him since, so I guess they must have kept him pretty busy as he's normally a very conscientious guy."

"It's possible, and even likely, that the killer changed out of this hoodie he's wearing in the picture into something else," said Odelia. "Which would make it impossible to identify him."

"Notice how you're referring to the killer as a he?" asked Laura with a smile. "You're automatically inclined to see him as a man, aren't you? It's the same with me. Though like Detective Kingsley says, it's perfectly possible that it was a woman."

"We think the killer may have escaped via the back exit," said Odelia. "You didn't see anyone sneak that way by any chance?"

Laura hesitated for a moment. "The thing is that we do sometimes see people leave that way. They see the sign and they think it's just another exit. We have to tell them they shouldn't go that way since it's for emergency situations only. But of course, we can't always be on hand to see them leave that way. I did see someone sneak out the back again this afternoon, though I couldn't tell you what time this was exactly. I was busy gathering up the clothes from the fitting rooms and putting them on hangers so I could put them back in the store. I would have said something about it, but then a customer asked me something about sizes, and by the time I was finished explaining, the other person was gone. And then frankly I completely forgot about it since it happens frequently."

"Can you show us this back exit?" asked Odelia.

"Of course. It's this way," said Laura and led us in the direction of the fitting rooms, which were located near the back of the store. We passed browsing shoppers busy taking clothes off the racks to try them on in the fitting rooms. The back exit was actually past the rooms, and if you didn't know it was there, you could easily miss it, as the sign that led there was obscured behind the section of fitting rooms. Probably this was on purpose so people wouldn't leave the store that way and grab a bunch of items without paying. This exit wasn't equipped with a pair of those vertical scanners you often see at the entrance of a store to prevent people from stealing stuff.

"And no cameras," said Chase as he scanned the ceiling all around.

"No cameras," Laura confirmed. "We probably should have cameras here and also the same scanners we have installed at the entrance of the store, since we're seeing more and more people sneaking out this way and grabbing a couple of items as they do. Without paying, of course." She grimaced. "It's odd that people who are on vacation and paying a lot of money to come on board the Ruritania still find it necessary to steal clothes from our boutique. You would think they can afford to pay for them, especially since everything in here is tax and duty-free."

"I think you probably get thieves everywhere," said Odelia.

"Just like you get murderers everywhere," Brutus added.

We glanced around, and I wondered if any pets would have seen the killer. It was very likely, for even as we looked around, I could see at least two lapdogs patiently waiting for their humans to finish trying on their clothes. So chances were that a dog had seen the killer and even got a good look at his face as he walked into the store, then presumably out through the back. But since it was now going on four o'clock, those shoppers and their dogs would long ago have moved to other stores or were back in their cabins. And since there were four thousand passengers on board, it was probably difficult to track the people who had been in the store at the time of the killer's presence.

Difficult, but not impossible. And as Chase and Laura checked the exit, Odelia crouched down next to us. "Clive promised he'd try and compile a list of passengers who were in the store at the time the killer was also in here," she told us. "And I asked him specifically to check for shoppers who were accompanied by their pets. So once I've got the list and the photo IDs of the people and their dogs, I want to pay a visit to these people. And while I do, I want you guys to talk to their pets. People usually don't pay a lot of attention to their surroundings, especially when they're shopping. But pets might. They might have been bored while their humans went from clothes rack to display table and tried on this or that garment. And they might have seen something unusual."

"Gotcha," I said, nodding. Clearly, Odelia and I thought alike, and it was a good idea to start with these people who owned pet dogs as we could talk to them while she talked to their owners. After all, we had to start somewhere, so we might as well start there.

Chase had finished checking out the exit but had found nothing of note. And since we were also part of the same mission, he opened the door for us so we could take a peek back there. It was a lot less spectacular than the Promenade. A narrow concrete corridor with subdued lighting that led in both directions and presumably led back to the main thoroughfare at some point. And as I glanced this way and that, I wondered suddenly if there wouldn't be any rats present. But try as I might, I couldn't detect their presence. They might have fled the ship, even though it wasn't sinking.

In other words, it was a dead end.

# CHAPTER 12

Our next port of call was the bar where Mrs. Davis had had a drink before she returned to her room, only a short half hour before she was eventually attacked and killed. The bartender was the same person who had been on duty when Maude Davis had sat at that very same bar having a drink. According to the footage we had seen of that moment, she had been in conversation with another passenger, but at some point their interaction must have turned acrimonious, for Mrs. Davis had slapped the man across the face and swept from the room. The other man had returned to his seat and had continued drinking steadily until he'd fallen off his stool and had to be carried off.

The bartender knew exactly who Chase and Odelia were referring to when they addressed him and showed him the printout from the CCTV camera that was discreetly located over the bar.

"Oh, I remember them," he said, nodding. "Yeah, they were real friendly at first, sitting close together and getting along pretty great. But then the woman wanted to return to her room, and the guy asked if he could tag along. She didn't like that. The guy then ordered more drinks until I felt he'd had enough. At which point he fell off his bar stool and I had to ask security to carry him back to his cabin to sleep it off." He shook his head. "We get a lot of drunks in here, as you can probably imagine, but very rarely this early in the day. But this guy, he just kept putting them away at a pace I've never seen before. As if he was used to the stuff, you know. But then maybe he was."

"You didn't catch a name, did you?"

"Nah, I didn't. But if you ask security, they'll have his cabin number. They like to keep track of people like this guy, just in case he causes more trouble further down the line. He'll be on their list."

Chase and Odelia thanked him for his time, and Chase then took out his phone and placed a call to the security center. Clive referred him to one of the security guards who had handled the contretemps, and moments later we were in conversation with the man who was still on duty and patrolling the Promenade with a colleague. Both men were dressed in casual touristy clothes: Hawaiian shirts and board shorts, and you would never guess they were security. But they were, making sure people behaved, stopping fights if necessary, and checking in with store security, which some stores had and some didn't, in case a shoplifter or pickpocket was caught red-handed.

Chase asked about the fight that Laura Rogers had referred to, and that her security guard had been called away for, and the security man confirmed it. Josh, as his name was, said the fight had been between two shoppers who couldn't decide who had gotten hold of a certain blouse that was on promotion first. They had started tearing each other's hair out, and then their spouses had also joined the fray, and the rest of the family too. It had turned into a big, nasty brawl, and security people from other stores had jumped in, and

Josh had to intervene to restrain people and make sure they didn't kill each other or destroy the interior of the store.

"Some of these people had obviously been drinking a lot," he explained with a slight grin. "Let's just say that things got pretty heated for a while. But we finally got it under control."

"So about this business at the bar," said Odelia, and showed Josh the picture.

"Oh yeah, I remember him," said Josh. "Now this guy was *wasted*. Couldn't stand or walk, so we had to carry him out. We checked for a room key card, so we would know where to take him. I think his name was Martin something. Just let me check..." He had taken out his phone and was reading a report he'd made. "Not Martin, Henry," he corrected himself. "Henry Morgan. Cabin 1034b, which is located on deck six aft. Judging by the state he was in, you might still find him passed out. We put him on his bed and made sure to leave a note to contact us when he woke up. He'll be on our watch list from now on, and we wanted to make sure he knew so this wouldn't happen again."

"Maude Davis, did she make a complaint about Mr. Morgan?" asked Odelia.

"She didn't. Not as far as I'm aware, at least. But according to the bartender, he had been making quite a nuisance of himself with the lady, which is one of the reasons we put him on our list of passengers to keep an eye on. If it happens again, he might even get banned, which would mean he'd have to leave the ship and return home under his own steam, which might get costly if he gets kicked off the boat on some remote island."

"Do people get banned from the Ruritania?"

"Oh, absolutely. If you don't follow the rules and regulations and become a nuisance to other passengers and the safety of the vessel, you can definitely get banned. Though it's the captain who has the final say, not us. To make sure we don't go around slapping people with bans at random."

"Of course."

Chase and Odelia thanked Josh for his help, to which the muscular guard replied that it was his pleasure. He clearly liked his job, and he was good at it as well.

The next half hour or so found us traversing the many corridors and stairwells on our way to Mr. Morgan, possibly the last person who had seen Maude Davis alive. Finally, we arrived at destination's end, by which point my paws were killing me. These cruise ships are huge, and if you don't know your way around, you could easily get lost, I'd imagine. Lucky for us, Josh had given us very clear instructions that Odelia and Chase had followed to the letter. Chase did the honors by knocking on Mr. Morgan's door. And when no reply came, he knocked again for good measure, adding a vocal admonition to open the door to the mix.

This time the door was finally opened, and a bedraggled figure stood before us. Judging from his appearance, he hadn't spent a pleasant afternoon after he had fallen off his bar stool.

"Henry Morgan?" asked Chase. "Ship security. Can we have a word, please, sir?"

"What is this about?" asked the man nervously as he glanced down at the four cats at Odelia's feet and blinked. I had the impression he thought he was suffering from delirium tremens and we weren't actually there.

"Let's take it inside," Chase suggested and didn't wait for a formal invitation but pushed past the man and into his cabin. It was pretty messy in there, I had to say, and the smell wasn't the most pleasant one I'd ever experienced. In fact, things smelled pretty moldy, as if something had died and was starting to decompose. I just hoped this wasn't our killer, and he hadn't stashed a couple of bodies in his bathroom or one of the closets.

The man sat down on the bed as he gave the large cop a look of apprehension. "Can you please tell me what it is you think I did?" he asked with a weak voice.

Chase produced the picture of Mr. Morgan with Maude Davis, and he stared at it with wide-eyed horror. Then he buried his face in his hands. "Oh no," he said. "She's gone and filed a complaint against me, hasn't she? I knew this would happen. Sexual harassment? Are you going to arrest me?" He looked up, bleary-eyed and definitely not looking his best. "I didn't touch her, I swear. Or at least I don't think I did. Things got a little hazy at some point as I probably drank too many appletinis. I should have stuck to apple juice, but then when they offered me an appletini, I couldn't say no in front of the lady since that would have been an admission that I'm an alcoholic, and I'm not. Twenty years sober." He pointed to a pin on his lapel. "Though as of this afternoon, I guess I'll have to reset the counter." He sighed deeply. "My daughters... can you please not tell my daughters? They're paying for my trip, you see, to celebrate the fact that I'm twenty years sober—or was."

"Nobody is telling anyone about this," Odelia assured the man. Clearly, she was feeling for him. "And we're not here to arrest you either."

"At least not yet," said Brutus.

"What did you and Mrs. Davis argue about?" asked Chase.

The man frowned as he tried to throw his mind back to that moment in the bar. "Um... we were getting along really well, you know. She said she was traveling alone, as her husband died last year. They used to go on cruises all the time, but then he died, and now she was taking the trip in honor of his memory. She told me she was traveling with his urn. Apparently, they also met on a cruise forty years ago, and she was going to scatter his ashes at the spot where they had met."

"Very romantic," Dooley commented.

"And since I'm also a widower, we had something in common and really got along well. But then an appletini came, and I had one and then another one, and I guess when she decided to return to her room, I got a little fresh under the influence of the appletinis, and so I asked if she wanted to join me in my cabin. That did not go down well. To say she was upset would be an understatement. We may have gotten along well, but clearly she wasn't interested to continue getting acquainted in a more private setting, and made that clear to me in no uncertain terms." He sighed deeply. "I must admit that I drank more appletinis after that, and maybe something stronger as well. Though I don't remember much of what happened after Maude left. I guess I felt bad about the way things had gone, and so..." He made a feeble gesture. "When I woke up, I was lying on this bed, so I guess someone must have put me here, removed my shoes, and even my pants."

"The bartender called security when you fell from your bar stool," Chase explained. "And they carried you back to your room."

"The thing is, Mr. Morgan," said Odelia gently, "that Maude Davis died."

He blinked a couple of times. "Died? What do you mean, died?"

"She was murdered," said Chase, not beating about the bush.

"Murdered!" said the man, looking thoroughly shocked now.

"And since you're possibly the last person who saw her alive, and you got into an argument with her, you can probably understand why we would be interested in having a little chat with you, sir."

Henry Morgan's face turned as white as the sheet he was sitting on. Then, as we watched on, his eyes turned up in his head, and he keeled over.

## CHAPTER 13

Chase seemed to have a sneaking suspicion that Henry Morgan was Maude's killer, but I could have told him this was highly unlikely given the time frame and the man's condition. Maude had left the bar at one-thirty to return to her cabin. We knew that Henry had stayed at the bar until a little before two o'clock, at which point he'd been carried off to his own cabin. So unless he'd made a miraculous recovery after the security people had deposited him on his bed, he wouldn't have been capable of murdering the woman. And besides, as sozzled as he was, he could never have made it past all of those cameras and then down to the Promenade to play peek-a-boo with the security cameras outside the store and abscond through the back exit. That certainly didn't seem physically feasible considering the state the man was in.

Unless he was faking it, of course, but the bartender had confirmed that he had downed so many appletinis that he couldn't possibly stand up straight. And I think Chase finally realized he was barking up the wrong tree, for as soon as they had managed to revive the guy, the cop was already adopting a less forceful tone with him. Whereas before he'd practically accused him point-blank of murder, now he simply told him to take it easy and to lay off the booze for the time being.

"You won't tell my girls, will you?" asked Henry anxiously. "I'll tell them in due course, but right now I don't want them to worry about me. They do that enough as it is, and have done so a lot over the years, as you can probably imagine with a dad who often used to be more drunk than sober."

"No, we won't tell them," Odelia said. "But you have to promise to take better care of yourself, Henry. You're no good to your daughters in this state."

"Thank you so much," said Henry, eyeing Odelia with an adoring look. Clearly, he'd just signed up for her fan club, if she would have had one.

I saw that Chase was staring at Henry's hand. "What happened to your hand?" he asked.

Henry held up the hand, where he had apparently sustained a nasty cut. "I'm not sure," the man confessed. "It must have happened when I fell off my bar stool. A piece of glass on the floor maybe."

Chase nodded, though he didn't look entirely convinced. But then part of a detective's training is to be suspicious, and he definitely looked suspicious now. But since it was unlikely that Henry was our guy, he decided not to pursue the matter.

We left the room after having ascertained that the man was comfortable and not in need of any medical assistance after his fainting spell. Though Odelia did impress upon him that he should probably go and see a doctor at the ship's medical center, just to make sure that this fainting business wasn't linked to some other underlying issue. And also to have this cut looked at.

As she closed the door, we pondered our next course of action for a moment. We didn't have long to wait, as Odelia had received a list of passengers with dogs that Clive had managed to compile. I don't know how he'd done it, but somehow he had. Apparently, he'd checked the footage before and after the killer had entered the store and had managed to extract images of most of the people entering the store. Then he had put them through their database of all the passengers they had on file and had put names to the faces somehow and come up with an extensive list. As Odelia and Chase studied the list, the cop heaved a deep sigh. The couple shared a look.

"If I'd known we would be working harder on vacation than back home..." said Chase.

"You heard what Madeline said," said Odelia. "She'll comp us our full stay. So we can take another cruise next year, all-inclusive and with the whole family."

"Let's pray there won't be any killers on board next time," said Chase fervently.

And so the work began. Most of these passengers would presumably not be in their cabins at that time, so it wasn't useful to adopt the approach of knocking on their doors. But they would be sitting down for dinner, and since every passenger had a card they needed to scan when they entered one of the dozen restaurants, at least we'd know where each of them would be at that time. And since it was coming up on dinner time, we wouldn't have long to wait to make the acquaintance of the half a dozen dogs that we needed to interview. Oddly enough, most of them were of a similar persuasion: Chihuahua, Pekinese, Maltese, Bichon Frisé, Yorkshire Terrier, Shih Tzu... I just hoped they wouldn't look down their noses at a couple of cats asking them a lot of questions.

But first, Odelia wanted to return to Maude's room. This business with the urn intrigued her for some reason, and she wanted to take a closer look at it. Call it a hunch, she told her husband, but she had a feeling that maybe something was there. Apart from the ashes of her dead husband, that is.

And so we soon found ourselves back in Maude's room. The body had been removed already and would be kept in a body bag at the ship's morgue located on the lowest deck until the proper authorities could board the vessel and launch their own inquiry. Since Maude died in international waters, that meant the country that had jurisdiction was the country the Ruritania was registered in, which was the US. So according to Madeline, that meant the FBI would presumably want to carry out an investigation since they had jurisdiction, and also Maude had been a US national, and mostly the FBI liked to conduct investigations into the murders of Americans traveling on cruise ships.

We arrived back at Maude's room, and Odelia and Chase put on their plastic gloves again and conducted a thorough search of the room. Oddly enough, of an urn there was not a single trace.

"Now where could that urn be?" asked Odelia finally as she studied a couple of paintings she had found shoved underneath the bed. They were nice paintings, all made by the same artist.

"You don't think the killer took it, do you?" asked Chase.

"Now who in their right mind would steal an urn?"

"Obviously, this person isn't in his right mind, or else he wouldn't have killed Maude."

"I think this is probably the work of a psychopath," said Dooley. "Or maybe he collects urns, that's also possible. Or both, of course. A psychopath who collects the ashes of dead people."

We all shivered as we imagined this guy wandering around the ship with Maude's urn.

"Or maybe he's one of Maude's husband's relatives who didn't approve of Maude scattering his ashes," Harriet opined. "Like a sister-in-law or a brother-in-law? The family wanted to give the man a proper burial on their family's plot of church land, only Maude had other plans. And now, before she could scatter his ashes, they decided to steal the urn and murder Maude in the process."

"It all sounds a little far-fetched," I said. "If they wanted to give their relative a proper burial, they could have simply gone to court. They didn't have to murder Maude while she was on this cruise and then steal the guy's ashes."

"I think we can all agree that murderers don't think straight," said Harriet, having become fond of her theory and sticking to it. "And so it wouldn't surprise me if that's exactly what happened. Though of course there could be other explanations," she reluctantly allowed.

"What do you think, Max?" asked Brutus, surprising me with his deference.

"I'm not sure," I said. "The fact that there was a struggle and that Maude had a chance to scream and pound the wall means there must have been some kind of argument between herself and the killer. And the fact that the urn is gone is probably significant, since it meant so much to her. So it is possible that the killer thought that Maude would be asleep, so he snuck into her room with the intention of stealing that urn. Only she woke up and started screaming, which is what David Adams next door heard. A fight broke out, and she died in the process, possibly because the killer was afraid her yelling and screaming would attract attention and someone would arrive to block him from leaving. But that's all pure speculation, since we don't have enough information yet."

It was perfectly possible that someone else had taken that urn, like a cleaning lady mistaking it for a trash can to throw out with the rest of the trash. Or maybe Maude didn't even carry that urn with her since basically we only had Henry's word for it that she had brought it along. Or she could have lied about it, wanting to impress the widower that he was. We simply didn't know.

And since the room didn't yield any other clues, much to Chase's chagrin, who muttered something about tons of clues going to waste for lack of a decent forensic team to dust for prints and look for the killer's DNA, we left, and Chase carefully locked the door and put the tape back in place that barred anyone from entering the room. The moment the FBI took over the case, they'd want to give that room a closer inspection and examine Maude's body. She might have some of the killer's DNA under her fingernails since she had fought the person, or other valuable information that could be gleaned. All in all, we were sailing blind, which was ironic since we were on a boat.

Chase and Odelia decided to return to the rest of the family, who were still by the pool, to talk to Gran but also to relax for a moment before dinner time. And since we'd all been on our paws for a while now, I have to say I was quite looking forward to some R&R. Not that a pool is my idea of fun, as I've already outlined in a different section of these chronicles of mine, but it definitely beat having to traipse all over the gigantic cruise ship for what felt like miles and miles.

We found the rest of the family by the pool. Grace was sound asleep, shaded from the sun underneath an umbrella. Uncle Alec and Charlene were also peacefully dozing, and Marge had almost finished her beach read. The only ones who seemed wide awake were Gran and Tex, the latter smearing sunscreen on the exposed parts of his physique, while Gran simmered quietly. The old lady did not look happy.

"She betrayed me, you know," she said the moment she laid eyes on us. "The two-timing jerk betrayed me. We were going to let the captain who isn't a captain decide, but before

I knew it, she took off with the guy. She's not my friend anymore, you hear me? Never again!"

"Uh-oh," said Harriet. "Sounds like trouble is brewing."

"This isn't good," said Dooley. "If Gran and Scarlett aren't friends anymore, that means she'll declare Scarlett's apartment off-limits to us, which means we won't be able to pay visits to Clarice."

Clarice is a formerly feral feline who had recently been adopted by Scarlett. And even though Scarlett had wanted to bring her along on this cruise, Clarice had put her paw down and said that she wasn't going anywhere near a boat. "Over my dead body!" she had declared more than once. So Scarlett had seen no other recourse than to leave Clarice with her grand-nephew Kevin and his family. They would take good care of her. Clarice hadn't been all that excited about the prospect, but it beat having to stay on a boat for ten days. And so it was decided. She had declared us all crazy for going along on the trip, but then I guess we're different that way.

"Did you have a fight with Scarlett?" asked Odelia now as she checked on Grace.

"A fight! If you can call being double-crossed a fight, then yeah, we had a fight. She didn't give me a chance to go anywhere near the guy. With her sexy wiles, she wrapped him around her little finger before I could even introduce myself. And then she just went off with him and totally forgot I even exist. Well, she can have him. But she will have lost a dear, dear friend of over fifty years."

She conveniently forgot the fifteen years she and Scarlett were sworn enemies, but then Gran often suffers from a selective memory. As it was, I had a feeling they would soon reconcile. At least I hoped so, for Gran and Scarlett fighting like cats and dogs could only lead to trouble.

"There's something we need to ask you, Gran," said Odelia now, after having ascertained that Grace wasn't too hot. The toddler was sleeping soundly, having exhausted herself playing in the pool all this time, first with her mom and dad, and then with her grandfather, who also looked pretty worn out, I have to say.

"If it's about Scarlett, I'm pleading the fifth," Gran grumbled.

"It's not about Scarlett," Odelia assured her. "It's about a woman who was murdered this afternoon."

This had Gran looking up. "Oh, that's right. Marge said you guys got roped into some kind of investigation again. So murder, huh?" She tsk-tsked freely. "I should have known this cruise ship would be a den of iniquity. Thieves and murderers and best friends who steal men from under your nose. It's even worse here than back home. At least nobody is trying to plant a knife in your back when you're not looking." She gave me the evil eye for some reason, and I recoiled a little. When Gran is upset, watch out!

"So we watched security footage of the killer, and we managed to track him to the boutique where you and Scarlett were at that time. In fact, you walked into the store less than a minute after the killer did. So there's a chance you may have come face to face with him. And I'm saying him, but it could also be a woman, of course."

"The female of the species is deadlier than the male," said Gran ominously. "And you only have to look at Scarlett for living proof of that." She studied the picture Odelia was showing her on her phone and frowned. "I don't remember seeing this person. Though of course there were a lot of people at the store. But for some reason, this hoodie he was wearing…" She zoomed in on the picture. "I'm not sure, but somehow I seem to have seen this hoodie before."

"It's possible the killer left it at the store," said Odelia. "He probably changed clothes before he walked out again. Or he could have escaped through the back exit, which isn't covered by CCTV, unfortunately."

Gran's brow creased as she tried to stir her recollection. "Have you been to the store?"

"Yeah, we were there. We interviewed Laura Rogers, who's the person in charge, but she didn't remember seeing anyone with this particular hoodie walking into the store. Though I can imagine that a hoodie like this would have drawn attention. When everyone is walking around in board shorts and Bermudas, someone dressed like this stands out."

"I wouldn't be too sure about that. Lots of people probably like to wear these hoodies. They're very popular, especially with kids. They think it makes them look cool or something. Gangsta, you know. So no, I don't think the killer would have stood out like a sore thumb. But like you said, he probably got rid of the hoodie the moment he walked into the store. Or maybe he made a beeline for the fitting rooms, dropped the hoodie in the hamper with returned clothes, changed into something else, and then walked out the back. And since there were so many people there, he wouldn't have stood out at all. Not unless he had some weird disfigurement or carrot-colored hair or something." She handed back the phone. "If I were you, I'd return to the store and look for the hoodie. Chances are it's still somewhere on the premises, and the police should be able to find the killer's DNA on it."

"Good thinking, Gran," said Odelia. "And I don't know why we didn't think of that."

Gran shrugged. "Because you're talking to an expert, honey. And if I wasn't so upset about what Scarlett did to me, I'd probably be able to solve this murder right here and now by simply using my little gray cells. But anger is clouding my judgment." And to show us she wasn't kidding, her face clouded, and she adopted a vicious look Maude's killer probably could have sympathized with.

## CHAPTER 14

Scarlett had to admit that Jack Harper proved excellent company. They had walked along the Promenade for a while, popping in and out of stores and generally getting to know each other a little better. Then they had sat down for a drink at one of the different eateries along the ship's main boulevard, with Jack ordering a flat white and Scarlett sticking to her usual cappuccino. Jack had commented on her figure and said she looked like a supermodel, a compliment she had returned by saying he didn't look too shabby himself. In fact, he reminded her of one of her favorite actors, which seemed to please Jack to no end.

"So what about your friend?" Jack asked as he took a sip from his flat white. "Didn't she want to tag along?"

"Oh, you know what they say," said Scarlett. "Two is company and three is a crowd. Vesta is here with her family, so I'm sure she's having a great time by the pool right now or going to the casino or enjoying a spa special." Which reminded her that she and Vesta had actually booked one of those spa specials, which looked really fun. But then, since she had met Jack, she figured she should probably spend time with him. How often did you meet a man like Jack Harper? Not that often!

"So Vesta is here with her family?" asked Jack.

"Yeah, her daughter and son-in-law are celebrating their twenty-fifth wedding anniversary, so the family all chipped in and got them this cruise since they've been wanting to go on one for ages."

"They're a big group, are they?"

"Um, well, there's Vesta, her daughter Marge and Marge's husband Tex, Vesta's son Alec and his fiancée Charlene, granddaughter Odelia and husband Chase, their daughter Grace, so... how many is that?"

"Eight," he said with a smile. "Not including you."

"Oh, and four cats," Scarlett added.

He arched an eyebrow. "Four cats?"

"Yeah, Vesta's family is big on cats, and they didn't want to leave them behind, so they asked the cruise line company, and they said they could bring them along, no problem. They're very clean animals."

"My God," said Jack, laughing. "Imagine traveling with four cats. I think I'd go nuts."

"Oh, but it's fine. They're used to it. Like I said, they're very big on cats."

They shared a smile, and she thought she had probably never met a more handsome man. He had the kind of distinguished gray hair that gave him personality. His beard was perfectly styled, and he also looked pretty buff, as if he worked out on a regular basis. "Can I tell you something funny?" she asked. "When we first saw you, we actually thought you were the captain. You were chatting with this woman, and we thought you were the captain, when in actual fact she was the captain, and you weren't. I have to say, you look a lot more like a captain than she does, though."

He smiled. "Thanks for the compliment. I'm not the

captain, though, and I wouldn't know the first thing about handling a vessel this size. I did once own a motorboat, and I was pretty proficient of handling her. But apart from that, nope. No captain's stripes for me."

"Do you know the captain? 'Cause you two seemed awfully friendly."

"No, actually I never met her before. But it's true that she's very nice. I think the moment you witnessed was when I was lying in her spot. She pointed this out to me, and after the initial awkwardness, we got along pretty well. She's a great person, and I think she does a terrific job managing this gigantic vessel and keeping us all safe from pirates and other marauders."

Scarlett stared at the man. "Pirates! Not really!"

"Oh, but of course. We are in the Caribbean, you know, which is well-known for its pirates." He grinned at her, and she slapped him lightly on the arm.

"You're scaring me, Jack!"

"I'm sure there used to be pirates, but that's a long time ago. These days, the only pirates you will meet are the ones trying to sell you stuff in any of the ports we visit."

"We were robbed this morning, though," Scarlett said. "Vesta and I? Someone got into our purses and stole our wallets and also our phones. Which is very annoying, I have to say."

"Oh, no," said Jack, giving her a look of distinct commiseration. "So what are you going to do?"

She shrugged. "I'm traveling with two cops, so I'm sure they'll handle it."

"Two cops?" he asked.

"Yeah, Vesta's son is our chief of police back home, and Odelia's husband is one of his detectives. So between the two of them, I'm sure they'll figure it out."

She could be mistaken, but a sudden coolness seemed to

descend on their pleasant conversation. Suddenly, Jack was downing his flat white in one gulp, glanced at his watch, and said, "Oh, shoot, is that the time? I'm sorry, Scarlett, but I've got to run. See you later, yeah? Bye."

And before she had a chance to say goodbye, he rocketed out of his chair as if something sharp or fiery had attached itself to the seat of his pants, and he was gone.

"But..." she said feebly, trying to locate him in the crowd of milling passersby and failing. "But where are you going?"

But Jack was gone. She wondered if it was something she said. Then she reflected that she had told him about Alec and Chase and wondered if Jack perhaps wasn't all that keen on officers of the law. But since essentially she was the type of person who could take the bad with the good, she finished her own drink and then walked along the Promenade in the opposite direction at a leisurely pace, before deciding to see if she could find her friend.

She arrived at the pool about ten minutes later and saw that Vesta's family was still where they had left them. Though when she got there, they were on the point of leaving.

"Oh, there you are," said Marge as she caught sight of Scarlett. "We were just wondering where you were. Are you joining us for dinner?"

"Of course," said Scarlett. She glanced around. "Where's Vesta?"

Marge and Tex shared a look of unease. "Um... I think she went back to the cabin," said Tex. "She said she wanted to change for dinner. Something about not feeling comfortable spending time at the captain's table looking like a tourist."

Scarlett laughed. "Typical Vesta. We are tourists, so why shouldn't we go dressed like them?"

Marge gave her a keen look, then said, "What happened between you and my mother this afternoon? When she got back here, she was very upset, and she had a lot of not-so-nice things to say about you."

"Oh, dear," said Scarlett. "It's probably because I took off with the captain."

"You took off with the captain?"

"Not the actual captain. We decided to approach him when we saw him in one of the boutiques along the Promenade, and since there are two of us and only one of him, we agreed that we would let him decide who he wanted to be with, you know. Only when he chose me, Vesta probably didn't like it, so now she's upset with me." She shrugged. "It will pass. It always does with her."

"I'm not so sure," said Marge. "She seemed really, really angry with you. She said some things that I probably shouldn't repeat, but the gist of it was that your friendship is over and that you're enemies once more. Which I sincerely hope is not the case, for the years that you and mom fought like cats and dogs were frankly very exhausting sometimes. She's not the easiest person to live with, you know, and when she's got a grudge against someone, it makes her even more insufferable."

"I wouldn't worry about it if I were you, Marge," Scarlett said. "Vesta and I have had our differences in the past, but from the moment we decided to put all of that behind us, we've been best friends, and I'm sure it will stay that way."

"I hope so," said Marge, directing a look of concern at her. "To me, you're part of the family, and I would very much like it to stay that way."

It warmed her heart to hear Marge say it, and the two women shared a hug.

"So what are your plans for tonight?" asked Scarlett.

"Um... I'm not sure yet," said Marge. "We were thinking about going to see a movie at the theater, but there's also a

Broadway show tonight. They're doing Mamma Mia, and I've always wanted to see that."

"You should go," said Scarlett. "It's your party, Marge, so whatever you decide goes, right?"

"Yeah, I guess so," said Marge. She looked troubled, Scarlett thought, and that just didn't do. "Look, Vesta and I will sort things out. You don't have to worry about us. You just have a great time with Tex."

"It's not that," said Marge. "Odelia and Chase got roped into a murder investigation, and now I'm concerned they'll spend the entire trip chasing suspects and gathering clues."

"A murder investigation? But how? When? Who?"

"A woman was murdered in her cabin this afternoon. And the captain asked Odelia and Chase if they could lead the investigation. At least until we arrive at the next port and the FBI can board the ship and take over. But since that'll be two more days, until then Chase is officially in charge."

"But doesn't the ship have its own security people?"

"It does, but apparently, the guy in charge isn't very capable at handling an inquiry like this. He jumped to the conclusion that the neighbor had done it and had the guy locked up in the brig before the captain got involved and they discovered that the guy couldn't have done it. So now the captain has decided to put Chase in charge. But I don't like it, Scarlett," she confessed. "I told Odelia I was fine with it, but on second thought… All this murder business? What if they get too close to the guy and he tries to murder them? They have a small child now and should be more careful about what they get involved in. A woman was murdered, and if the killer feels cornered, I'm sure he won't hesitate to strike again. And then maybe Grace won't have a mom or a dad anymore, and I…" Her voice broke. "I won't have a daughter or a son-in-law."

She rubbed Marge on the back. "I'm sure they'll be careful," she said. "And also, they've got the cats to look after them, right?"

But when Marge gave her a dubious look, it was clear she didn't think their cats were a match for a murderer once he decided to get rid of the detectives on his trail. Which is when she was suddenly reminded of Jack Harper's strange reaction when she mentioned she was traveling with no less than two police officers. Could that have triggered him into suddenly taking off like that? But that could only mean one thing. That Jack was in trouble with the law somehow. Or maybe... he was the killer?

## CHAPTER 15

Whether Marge and Tex would see a movie that night, take in a Broadway show, or gaze at the stars at the stargazing event on the observation deck didn't matter all that much to me. What did matter was that dinner time had finally arrived, and since I was starving, I was happy for the respite. Then again, dinner time also meant we'd have to interview potential canine witnesses, so I wasn't sure how much we would be able to enjoy our dinner.

Our humans collected their things and all moved to their respective cabins, which were located in the same section of the ship. Marge and Tex shared a room, of course, and also Chase and Odelia and Grace. And Uncle Alec and Charlene had their own cabin. The problem was that Vesta and Scarlett also shared a cabin, but with the rift that seemed to have developed between the two former friends, that might not be advisable now. Though according to Scarlett, the rift could easily be resolved.

We followed our humans as they traversed the different decks and found their way through the maze of corridors and stairwells until we finally arrived at our destination. We waited with bated breath as Scarlett knocked on her own cabin door, then inserted her key into the lock and swung open the door. Seated on the bed was Vesta, and she didn't even deign Scarlett a look. There were two beds in the room, one occupied by Gran and the other one by Scarlett. The latter now entered the room, the family waiting in the corridor, just in case things got ugly and they had to intervene.

But as we watched, Gran suddenly spoke up. "Scarlett Canyon, there's something I have to tell you and I want you to listen very carefully. You have hurt my feelings something terrible. You have stepped on my heart and ground it into the dirt with hobnailed boots. You have yanked my soul from my chest and spat on it." At this, she turned around to face her friend. "And so I figured our friendship was at an end and we were mortal enemies once more. But then I got to thinking. These last couple of years have been a lot of fun spending time with you. I enjoy having a best friend like you in my life, and frankly, I wouldn't want to go back to the old days of fighting tooth and claw all the time. So, I have decided to find it in my trampled and bruised old heart to try and forgive you. Though if you want to offer me an apology right now, that would be very welcome because I'm not sure I'm taking the correct approach here since a part of me wants to tear you limb from limb and feed your mutilated carcass to the sharks, of which I've been told there are plenty in these waters."

Scarlett, who had put a hand to her own heart, perhaps not as tattered and torn as her friend's, now spoke. "I do want to apologize, Vesta. If I've hurt your feelings, I'm sorry. I never meant to choose Jack over you, but when he showed an interest in me, I guess my ego was boosted to such an extent that I totally forgot how much more important our friendship means to me than the company of a man. And besides, I don't think he's as great as he pretended to be. In actual fact, I think he just might be that killer Odelia and Chase have been looking for."

At this, Odelia produced an audible intake of breath, and Chase softly cursed.

Gran offered her friend a smile. "Only you could attract the attention of a guy and then find out he's a murderer. Come here." And she got up from the bed with surprising alacrity and enveloped her friend in her arms. And as a sigh of relief went through the collected company, I think we all breathed a little easier knowing that the famous feud as it had existed between these two old ladies wouldn't see a reprisal. Frankly, I don't think I could go through all that again.

"You didn't tell us that you met a killer, Scarlett," said Marge.

"Yeah, you could have told us about this... Jack, is it?" said Chase.

"I'm not sure he is a killer," said Scarlett. "But when I mentioned that you are a cop, and that Alec is our chief of police, he couldn't get away from me fast enough. Which got me thinking that maybe he's been up to something. And then when Marge told me about this murder you guys are investigating..."

"What's the guy's name?" asked Chase, taking out his notebook.

"Jack Harper. He looks like a captain but he's assured me he's not."

"He's very handsome," said Gran. "He's got such a nice beard."

"The most gorgeous beard. Like a movie star. Or a captain."

"A movie star who plays a captain."

"Or a captain who plays a movie star."

"Or a murderer," said Chase dryly. "Okay, I'll liaise with

the security team and ask them to pick this Jack Harper up for questioning."

This small matter resolved, our humans got ready for dinner, and the four of us sat around and waited more or less patiently. The odd thing about humans is that they need a lot of time to get ready for anything. Marge calls it making herself look presentable, while Gran refers to it as putting on her war paint, whatever that means. The nice part about being a cat is that we never have to put on any war paint and that we're always ready, and we don't even need to take a shower or put on our best clothes or try to make ourselves look more beautiful than we are. We're like the stuff you buy on the internet: we work out of the box.

Half an hour later, the final member of our select company was finally ready, and so we went in search of a restaurant to enjoy dinner. And since Chase wanted us to pursue the leads he and Odelia had worked out, he convinced his family to mix business with pleasure and select the restaurant where most of the pets we needed to talk to would be gathered according to the ship's database. Marge and Tex, even though they had expressed their reservations about this investigation, went along with the idea, even though Uncle Alec seemed to have a different idea in mind. He had his sights set on a restaurant where they served delicious ribs, from what he'd gleaned from a person he met by the pool, and so he and Charlene would check out the ribs while we looked for a murderer. To each their own, I guess. And the Chief probably had a point. Even though Chase decided to work while on vacation, that didn't mean Uncle Alec had to do the same. He had expressed a fervent wish not to get involved in any of this and to switch off completely, and that was his prerogative.

We arrived at the restaurant in question, which was of the Italian variety, with plenty of pasta and pizza on the menu, and I hoped they would have some tasty morsels for cats on the menu as well. As far as I could tell, we were the only cats on board the vessel, and everywhere we passed, people looked surprised, almost as if they had never seen a cat before in their lives.

"We attract a lot of attention, don't we, Max?" said Dooley.

"We sure do," I said, after a couple had done a very expressive double-take when they saw us pass in Odelia's wake.

"I think it's because most people don't travel with cats," said Brutus. "They only travel with dogs. But then Odelia isn't a normal person."

"Odelia is not normal?" asked Dooley. "In what sense?"

"Well, for one thing, she can talk to us," said Brutus. "And for another, she insists on taking us along wherever she goes, whereas most people simply dump their pets someplace to get rid of them when it's not convenient."

"I don't like that practice very much," Harriet confessed. "These places, these pet hotels or whatever you want to call them, it's just not the same as being with your own humans, is it?"

"No, it sure isn't," I agreed. We had arrived in the main dining room, and our humans took a seat at a table while we awaited further developments. Before long, they had decided what they were going to have, and Odelia decided what we were going to have, and then the big maneuvers commenced. It wasn't one of those restaurants where a person comes by with a little notepad and jots down your food items of choice and delivers it to your table. No, this was a self-service restaurant, and so our humans proceeded to line up at the long buffet while they loaded their trays with whatever they had selected. Before long, the table was almost as laden with food items as the buffet, and as the family tucked in, separate plates were positioned on the floor and pieces of meat added for our benefit. And since I was basically starving, I attacked the food with relish. By the time the manna from heaven finally dried up, I had eaten my fill, and so had my friends. And since we had been given our marching orders, we started looking around for those pets we could engage in conversation. Now that I had some food in me, I looked upon the world with renewed vigor.

The four of us decided to split up, with Dooley and I covering one half of the restaurant, and Brutus and Harriet covering the other half. And so we talked to several pets of the canine variety, but none of them had much of interest to share. It wasn't until we locked onto a small, so-called sausage dog or Dachshund that we finally seemed to be getting somewhere.

"Hey there," I told the sausage dog.

The tiny dog looked up and seemed to wonder where we had suddenly sprung from, for she said, "Cats? I didn't even know cats were allowed on this boat."

"Well, not only are we allowed, our presence is encouraged," I said.

"Yeah, cats are important," said Dooley. "We provide a cozy atmosphere to any place we are inserted into, and we put smiles on people's faces with our madcap antics."

We shared a wink and would possibly also have shared a high-five, but that seemed to be overdoing things. The Dachshund didn't seem convinced. "I don't like cats," she revealed, causing us to wonder if she was a member of the anti-cat brigade in the town she hailed from.

"You don't like cats?" I asked.

"No, I most certainly do not," said the Dachshund decidedly. She held up a paw and showed us the underside where I saw a long red scar. "See this? A cat did that. Just like that. Unprovoked attack. I don't know what it is about cats, but for some reason, they like to attack you when you least expect it." She now held up her front paws in a pugilistic stance. "But this time you won't get the satisfaction. I've learned karate, and if you come anywhere near me, I'll strike!"

"Oh, but we're not like that," I assured the doggie. "We don't hit or scratch innocent little doggies like yourself. In fact, we're all for inter-species friendship. Our neighbors are dogs too. One is a sheepdog, and the other is a Yorkshire Terrier, and we get along with both of them very well."

"They're very good friends of ours," said Dooley. "Even though they're members of dog choir and prefer associating with other dogs. But we don't hold it against them since we mostly associate with other cats ourselves."

"Well, you're warned," said the Dachshund, as she didn't relax her vigilance even for a single moment. "You touch me, you die," she added, elucidating her position.

"Okay, so we won't touch you," I said, figuring that would be a nice compromise that we could all live with. "So the thing is, a woman was murdered this afternoon, and our humans are conducting an investigation. So we would like to ask if you happened to notice anything out of the ordinary when you were at the Bella Bello boutique with your human this afternoon. We know you were there since we've got you on camera. And since the killer entered the same store around the time you were there, we were wondering if maybe you would have seen him by any chance?"

We both looked at the doggie expectantly, and I won't conceal the fact that I was hoping, sincerely hoping, she would give us something—anything—that might help us identify this killer.

But the Dachshund shook her head. "I'm sorry," she said finally. "But I'm not in the habit of assisting cats in their inquiries. So if you could please move along now? You're disturbing me at a time when my digestive system needs to be working overtime."

"So you haven't seen this killer, or you're simply not interested in helping us find him?" I asked, wondering how the Dachshund's position could accurately be described. Insulting to cats as a species? Maybe. Hindering a police investigation? Possibly. Canine arrogance? Absolutely.

"I may have seen something," the dog allowed. "But like I said, I don't negotiate with cats, and that's my final word on the matter. So please leave."

Dooley and I shared a look of surprise. We had talked to a lot of different pets over the course of our many investigations, but it rarely happened that a pet simply refused to cooperate. And since it was hard to wrap my head around it, I decided to try a different approach. "So... you don't care that a woman was murdered? I mean, it could have been your human, you know. This murderer could have entered any cabin and unleashed his homicidal tendencies on a passenger."

"No killer would ever come close to my human," said the dog with a sort of smirk on her face. "For the simple reason that my human has a black belt in karate. And if this killer ever came anywhere near her, she would simply chop him in two like a twig."

"She can do that?" asked Dooley, surprised. "A human can chop another human in two like a twig?"

"Oh, absolutely," said the dog, momentarily forgetting her strict policy about never engaging a cat in conversation. "She can also chop a brick in two. She produces this awfully loud yell, brings down her hand, and moments later the brick realizes it's done for and falls down into two pieces on the floor. It's pretty awesome." The little doggie almost became animated as she discussed her human's karate chops, but then she suddenly remembered her strict anti-cat position and became terse again. "Not talking," she said, producing the universal sign of zipping up her lips.

"Okay, fine," I said. "So you probably don't want to know about the dog snatcher that's loose on the ship either." And I started to walk away.

I hadn't taken three steps before she cried, "Wait! What dog snatcher!"

"Oh, just this mysterious creature that's been roaming the ship at night. It carries this big burlap sack and snatches up any dog it can find."

"But, but, but... That's bad!" said the doggie, and I could see how her tail was actually trembling. "They can't do that. This person should be stopped!"

"What can you do?" I said. "Most people don't care about dogs, you see. They just figure one more dog in dog heaven is fine, as long as they can have their fun and participate in the on-board entertainment that's being provided. So if tonight you suddenly hear a rustling sound behind you, run, run like the wind. For it's probably the dog snatcher out to get you and chop off your head."

"Chop off my head!"

"That's what he does. He collects heads of doggies like you and puts them in his bag."

"What does he do with the heads?" asked Dooley. "And why does he only collect the heads and not the rest?"

"Um... well..."

"Is it because he likes doggie brains?"

I pointed at my friend. "That's it. The doggie snatcher is also a zombie, so he needs a constant supply of doggie brains to keep him going. He used to be a dog himself, you see, but since he was transformed into a zombie, he craves brains and needs to keep feeding himself."

The doggie was gulping a little at this and glanced around uncertainly, as if expecting the zombie dog snatcher to pop up any moment. "Okay, so maybe I did see something odd this afternoon," she admitted. "If I tell you what it was, will you promise to warn me when you see the dog snatcher?"

"Absolutely," I said. "Cats have a sixth sense about dog snatchers. So the moment we sense his presence, we'll give you a heads-up."

"So we were at the store, Mirna and me..."

"By the way, what is your name?" I asked. "I'm Max, and this is Dooley."

"Frank," said the doggie, even though she didn't look like a Frank to me. "So we were at this store, and suddenly this man walked up to me who had this crazy look in his eyes. The look of a killer, just as you say, Max. For a moment there, I really thought he was going to attack me, you know. But then at the last moment, he veered off course and went the other direction, heading straight for the back of the store. Moments later, he was gone, and he didn't return."

"Was he wearing a hoodie?" I asked.

"He was," Frank confirmed. "And he had this wild look in his eyes. Really crazy eyes." She suddenly gasped. "Was it... was it the dog snatcher, Max?"

"Possibly," I allowed.

"Your human would have protected you," Dooley pointed out. "With her black belt in karate, she would have chopped this dog snatcher into little pieces before he had a chance to come anywhere near you. Isn't that right, Max?"

"Well, considering the person you saw was probably Maude Davis's killer, he had other things on his mind," I said. "What did this man look like, Frank?"

"Well, he was big, and he had this round face and this big nose in the middle of that round face, and he had a big belly underneath that hoodie of his that he was wearing." She thought for a moment. "Yeah, that's about it."

"A big man with a big face, a big nose, and a big belly," Dooley said, summing it up succinctly.

"Probably from eating all of those doggie brains," said Frank with a shiver.

Dooley had been studying the sausage with interest. "Why did your human name you Frank, Frank? It's not usually a girl's name."

Frank shrugged. "I guess she doesn't know I'm a girl. She seems to think I'm a boy."

Dooley nodded seriously. "Humans," he said. "They may know karate, but that doesn't mean they're smart."

"Oh, I don't mind, you know. Though she does keep trying to hook me up with our neighbor's dog, who's also a Dachshund and also a girl. They seem to think we'd make a nice couple and make lots of puppies. I keep telling her that's not gonna happen, but she simply won't listen."

We decided to thank her for the information and leave her be, for her human had noticed us and was darting annoyed glances in our direction. And if what Frank had told us was true and her human was fond of karate and chopping things in two, I thought it was probably best to remove ourselves from her presence. I don't know about you, but I don't enjoy being karate-chopped.

## CHAPTER 16

"Why did this man want to attack Frank, Max?" asked Dooley.

"I'm sure he didn't want to attack Frank, Dooley," I said. "But you have to remember that he had just murdered a woman, and he was eager to make a clean getaway, so he probably wasn't paying all that much attention to Frank. She simply was in the way as he made a beeline straight for the fitting rooms, where he could get rid of his outfit and put on different clothes and head out the back."

"There's one thing I don't understand," he said.

"What's that?"

"Why would a man who snatches dogs, chops off their heads, and eats them also be a murderer of middle-aged ladies on cruise ships? Or maybe he decided to try something different for a change and was going to chop off Mrs. Davis's head as well but changed his mind at the last minute?"

"That story about the dog snatcher is just something I made up, Dooley," I explained. "Because Frank didn't want to help us, so I decided to invent that story to make her more cooperative. And it worked, for she gave us a description of a man who could very well be Maude Davis's killer."

Dooley gave me a strange look, and if I didn't know any better, I would have said he was upset with me. Then his next words confirmed this view. "You shouldn't have done that, Max," he said. "You shouldn't have lied to that poor Frank and made her so scared."

"But it was just a strategy," I said. "To make her more cooperative."

"But she was scared, Max. And now she will look under her bed tonight and be afraid that the dog snatcher will be lurking there, ready to chop off her head and eat her brains."

"Oh, Dooley," I said. I could have explained to him how sometimes the end justifies the means, but I had the feeling it wouldn't go down well with my friend.

"I would very much like you to apologize to her, Max. And tell her that the boogie man doesn't exist and that she doesn't have to be afraid that he will chop off her head and eat it."

"Not now, Dooley. We have other witnesses to interview and—"

But it was obvious that he felt it was important that we put the situation right. And so, in the end, I gave in and we retraced our steps to find ourselves back at the same table, with the same karate chopper and Frank, the female sausage dog.

"I know what you're going to say, Max," she said. "But I've already taken my precautions. When the dog snatcher shows up, I'm going to jump on my human's lap, and she will protect me, I'm sure."

"That's just the thing, Frank," I said. "That dog snatcher? He doesn't exist. I made him up just so you would talk to us."

"And..." Dooley prompted.

"And I sincerely apologize for the inconvenience my words may have caused."

"I don't understand," said Frank. "The dog snatcher, he's real, right?"

"No, he's not. He never was real. He's just a figment of my imagination to make you talk to us about this man you saw."

Frank studied me for a moment, but when she decided that I was serious, she frowned. "That wasn't very nice of you, Max."

"I know," I said.

"It wasn't nice of Max," Dooley pointed out, "but it was still better than scratching you and leaving a nasty scar on your paw."

"Yeah, I guess you're right," she said. "But still. Now you made me scared, and I don't like to be scared. And also, if I'd jumped on my human's lap, she probably wouldn't have liked it, and then she would have gotten upset with me and wondered what was going on. And since I can't explain it to her, it would have created this awkward situation that wouldn't have been a lot of fun."

"Like I said, I'm sincerely sorry," I said, and I meant it, too. I probably could have found some other method of extracting the information from her, without scaring her out of her wits. Then again, what was done was done, and I couldn't change what had happened.

"I guess Dooley is right, though," said Frank. "Telling a fib is probably better than scratching me for no reason at all." She gave me a magnanimous look. "I forgive you, Max. You did what you thought was right and I can appreciate you coming back here and apologizing. That took guts."

"Well…"

I saw her tail was wagging happily, and clearly the trauma had passed. "I didn't believe you, you know. About that dog snatcher? I knew you were pulling my paw, but I figured I'd play along."

"Okay."

"Dogs are a lot smarter than cats, you see. We can see you coming from miles away."

"You can?" asked Dooley, much intrigued. "I didn't know that."

"Oh, absolutely. I have eyes like an eagle and a nose like… like… Well, a pretty good nose."

"So that's why you saw Maude Davis's killer," said Dooley. "Because of your eagle eyes."

"Absolutely," said Frank, and she was glowing like a Christmas tree with pretty satisfaction.

And as we left the doggie, I felt much easier in my mind about having come clean to her about that doggie snatcher. Sometimes you have to simply swallow your pride and do the right thing.

Frank was the last dog in our section of the restaurant, and so we circled back to our own table and met up with Brutus and Harriet, who had also just returned from their mission.

"And?" asked Brutus. "What did you discover?"

"Well, we talked to this one dog who seems to have clapped eyes on a man who could very possibly be our killer," I said. "Though of course it could have been someone else." But my hunch told me that it might very well have been the killer Frank had seen. "You?"

"Nothing," said Brutus. "A lot of these dogs are too big for their boots and won't even talk to us."

Dooley laughed at this. "But Brutus, dogs don't wear boots." He turned to me. "Do they, Max?"

"Well, some dogs wear booties in the winter," I said. "When they go outside and they need to protect their paws when they have to tinkle."

"Max found a way to make dogs talk," Dooley now revealed. "He invented a story about a dog snatcher, and it made the last dog we talked to sing like a canary, didn't it, Max?"

"Um…"

"But since I didn't think it was fair to scare that poor dog out of her senses, Max apologized and told the dog that the dog-snatching zombie doesn't exist and that her brains are perfectly safe."

"We did talk to a couple of dogs," said Harriet. "But none of them seemed to have seen anything out of the ordinary."

"One of them saw a man dressed like Santa," said Brutus. "He thought it could have been the killer. But I told him it was highly unlikely. He seemed disappointed since he said he had ambitions of becoming a police dog, and asked if we could put in a good word with our humans so he could enter police academy."

"It's very tiring, all this interviewing," said Harriet. "I think we probably deserve extra compensation now." She had directed these words at our human, who had been listening intently without seeming to do so. A lot of people still think it's a little weird when humans talk to their cats. Then again, most pet owners talk to their pets all the time, only they don't expect an answer.

"So this guy you said this dog saw," Odelia said now, "what did he look like, exactly?"

And so I gave her the description Frank had given us. She seemed very happy with this and patted me on the head for my efforts, then proceeded to fill our plates once again as a token of her appreciation. Now don't get me wrong, I don't mind the odd cuddle or pat on the head from time to time, but in my opinion the best way to express your gratitude is to offer food. You can never go wrong with food. It could just be me, of course, because eating is one of my favorite hobbies.

Odelia passed the information we had gleaned onto her husband, who jotted down a couple of notes in his notebook. All in all, I thought we may have made some progress in the case. Though how they were going to identify a guy who answered to such a vague description was beyond me. So among the four thousand people on board the Ruritania we were looking for a large man with a round face, a big nose and a big belly. That probably described about half of the male passengers.

But Odelia didn't seem to think this was a mission impossible at all. On the contrary, she eagerly started expounding to her uncle about how they would probably be able to nab this guy before the FBI got there and took the case out of their hands.

But then Odelia has always been an inveterate optimist.

## CHAPTER 17

Conversation at the dinner table had turned lively again. Odelia and Chase had been discussing their case with the rest of the family, and since one way or another the whole family had a keen interest in these cases they often got involved in, everyone chipped in to offer their opinion. Odelia obviously thought it might yield some information she and Chase hadn't thought of, since the collected wisdom was extensive.

Her dad offered the medical angle. "Maybe Maude Davis was ill, you know, and she hired this man to kill her. It happens!" he added when a howl of disapproval rose up around the table. "People have been known to contract their own murderers to have themselves murdered. Sometimes they do it for life insurance reasons, but other times simply because they lack the courage or the knowledge to do it themselves. And if this Maude Davis had recently become a widow, maybe she was in a state of distress and eager to join her husband on the other side of the veil."

"It's possible," Uncle Alec allowed, "but you have to admit it's highly unlikely, Tex. If she wanted to die, there are probably easier ways to do it than to hire a murderer and have herself strangled. By all accounts, it's a slow and painful death, and not one Mrs. Davis would have wished for herself." He turned to Chase. "What do you know about her antecedents? Anything that might have a bearing on the case?"

"Well, we do have some information," said Chase. "Maude Davis was a widow, as we have already ascertained. She lost her husband last year. I talked to Maude's sister and she filled in some of the details. Clark Davis was a retired circus owner, who had worked all his life as the director of his own circus. Maude was a trapeze artist, who later became his wife. But since it's tough for circuses everywhere, and people aren't as keen as they used to be to pay to watch clowns throw cream pies in each other's faces or to see a lion tamer stick his head in a big cat's mouth, Clark decided to close the circus five years ago and start training animals instead. And he was doing okay, working out of a zoo in West Los Angeles and training animals for the movie industry, when tragedy struck last year and he unexpectedly died after a short illness. As a consequence, Maude was forced to sell up, and she took a job as a zookeeper, working under the new management."

"That must have been hard," said Charlene commiseratingly. "First to lose your husband in such a tragic way, and then having to sell his life's work and having to work for the new owners."

"I think she was okay with it," said Chase. "Maude's sister said she was happiest when she worked with her big cats. And she sold the zoo to Clark's cousin, a guy called Blake Sooms, who owns several zoos, so it's not as if she was selling her soul to the devil. She was glad someone was going to take care of the animals. That was the main thing with Maudie, as her family called her."

Dooley had turned to me. "I don't understand, Max."

"What don't you understand, Dooley?"

"Well, Maude Davis was allergic to cats. But she loved working with big cats."

"It's possible to be allergic to cats and not to big cats," I explained. "It all depends on the person."

"Maybe Maude liked her big cats so much she was prepared to suffer to enjoy the privilege of their company," Harriet suggested. "Like artists who like to suffer for their art? *Moi*, for instance."

I wondered how Harriet had ever suffered for her art, but decided not to open a can of worms by broaching the sensitive subject.

"Any idea if the zoo angle has any bearing on what happened to Maude?" asked Charlene.

"Not really," Chase admitted. "As far as I can tell, she made this trip by herself, not accompanied by friends or relatives, so nobody on board would have known her. It might simply be a case of a break-in gone wrong. It might even be Captain Invisible. In spite of what Madeline told us about his MO being that he favors violence-free crimes, it's always possible he broke into Maude Davis's room, she surprised him, and he reacted with violence to shut her up. It wouldn't be the first time that a thief suddenly becomes a murderer when he's being caught and is afraid of going to jail."

"The weird part is that the urn with her husband's ashes has gone missing," said Gran. "That's what you said, right, Odelia?"

"Yeah, the ashes don't seem to be in the room anymore," Odelia confirmed. "Though we only have Henry Morgan's word for it that they were ever there in the first place."

"Maude's sister did mention something about that urn," said Chase as he consulted his notebook. Clearly, the cop had been busy. "She said that Maude had mentioned Clark's dying wish. Though she didn't go into specifics, Maude's sister believes she could have been referring to the man's ashes. They always shared the story of how they met during a cruise on one of the Caribbean islands in the area and how they had always vowed to go back there one day. So it's definitely possible she brought the urn along to scatter his ashes on this island."

"It's a very romantic story, isn't it, Max?" said Dooley.

"I guess so," I said.

"I don't think it's very romantic to scatter a person's ashes," said Harriet with a shiver. "I mean, imagine if you get some of that stuff in your face? Or worse, in your mouth? There's nothing romantic about chewing on a person's dead remains, Dooley."

"Well, I still think it's romantic," Dooley insisted. "And I hope that when I'm gone, you guys will scatter my ashes in a place that's meaningful to me."

"So what is a meaningful place for you, Dooley?" I asked.

"Oh, I don't know," said Dooley. "My litter box, maybe? I've spent many happy hours in that litter box, so it's very meaningful to me."

"We're not going to scatter your ashes in your litter box, Dooley," said Brutus. "For one thing, litter is supposed to be thrown away, not kept as a memento of a person who died. And for another, you're the youngest of the four of us, so if anyone is going to scatter your ashes, it won't be us."

"So who will it be?" asked Dooley, much intrigued.

"Let's not go into all of that," Harriet suggested. "For now, we're all happy and healthy, and I would very much like to keep it that way. So let's not talk about scattering any ashes, all right?"

At the table, the conversation continued unabated. "It's always possible that some former colleague of Maude's joined the trip and had some old score to settle," Scarlett suggested. "After all, if she and her husband worked at this circus for all those years, there may have been bad blood, especially if they were forced to give it up."

"It's a good point," Charlene agreed. "These old grudges can be terrible. I once had to fire one of the secretaries for not doing her job, and when I met her again six months later, she cut me in public. Simply crossed the street and pretended not to see me!"

"Ignoring a person is not the same thing as murdering them," Uncle Alec pointed out.

"Well, I know that, but still. I was shocked when she simply crossed the street the moment she saw me coming. She even hid her daughter's face so she wouldn't see me. The gall of the woman."

"It is true that an old grudge could be at the heart of this case," said Marge. "But how are you ever going to find out? You would have to interview all of Maude and Clark Davis's old circus colleagues and see if one of them is particularly upset that the circus was closed down."

"Or Chase and Odelia could simply reference the names of these old circus colleagues with a list of passengers," Uncle Alec suggested. "It wouldn't be hard. The hardest part would be to collect the names of circus performers."

"We could always ask Maude's sister," said Chase. "She probably has access to that kind of information. Though if someone snuck on board the ship with the express purpose of murdering Maude, chances are that they used a false name."

"Yeah, I guess you're right," said Uncle Alec. He leaned back and placed his napkin on the table. "I think you should probably leave the investigation to the FBI. They've got the resources and the contacts. They can ask their field agents in Los Angeles to investigate the circus angle while they get a medical examiner to look at the body and a forensic team to go through that room of the woman with a fine-tooth comb. Also, the hoodie. Have you found the hoodie yet?"

"No, we haven't," said Odelia. "I returned to the boutique to ask, but Laura Rogers said she hadn't come across any hoodies. And when I looked myself, I didn't find one either. But if this killer is smart, he wouldn't have left his hoodie behind, which must be riddled with his DNA. And I do think he's smart. Very smart."

"Yeah, he won't make it easy for us," said Chase.

"All the more reason to leave the investigation to the FBI," Uncle Alec argued. "At least then you two can enjoy your vacation. Not to mention allowing Tex and Marge to celebrate their wedding anniversary without having to worry about you guys hunting a murderer."

Marge gave her daughter a keen look. "Your uncle is right, honey. You should leave this to the FBI. It's far too dangerous to look for this killer yourselves."

But judging from the set look on Odelia's face, I didn't think that advice from her mom and her uncle would resonate. Odelia might be the sweetest person on the planet, always ready to give us whatever our little hearts desire, but she has a stubborn streak, especially when it has to do with her work. And so I very much doubted she'd give up. She wanted to catch this guy, and also the guy who had robbed her, if it was the last thing she did. I just hoped it wouldn't be the last thing she did!

## CHAPTER 18

Odelia hadn't forgotten about Scarlett's hunch that her 'captain,' Jack Harper, might be involved in the murder of Maude Davis, or at the very least that he might be Captain Invisible. So after dinner, while the others went to see Mamma Mia, she and Chase decided to pay the guy a visit in his cabin. And since I'm not all that into Broadway musicals, or even off-Broadway musicals, or off-off-Broadway musicals, I decided to tag along, and so did the rest of our foursome.

"Don't you want to see Mamma Mia?" I asked Harriet.

"Max, I like to sing, but that doesn't mean I necessarily like to watch others sing," she said. "And besides, I've seen the movie, so I'm fine."

"It's not the same thing," I told her. "There's probably a big difference between watching a movie and watching a live performance of a show. When you can see the actors live on stage and hear them singing their—"

"Max, it's fine!" she said emphatically, making it perfectly clear that as far as she was concerned, the topic was closed.

"Okay, all right," I said. "So no Broadway show for you."

Once we had left the restaurant and our humans set a course for the cabin where Jack Harper was staying, Brutus hung back and said quietly, "She didn't talk about anything else but that musical the week before we departed. But then she found out that Shanille has decided to set up a performance of Mamma Mia next season and that she is organizing an audition for the main roles, and so now she doesn't want to have anything to do with this whole Mamma Mia anymore."

"Why? Because she's afraid Shanille won't pick her?"

"No, because she feels she shouldn't have to audition in the first place. She figures that as the undisputed star of cat choir, Shanille should have given her the main role like that, without going through this whole rigmarole of auditions."

"Oh, I see. And now she's going to boycott Mamma Mia?"

"She is going to boycott Mamma Mia," Brutus confirmed. "Which means I will also have to boycott Mamma Mia, and if you and Dooley know what is right for you, you will also boycott Mamma Mia. In fact, any cat who joins the show will automatically become Harriet's worst enemy, and that includes Shanille herself."

"God," I said. "Maybe Shanille should just give the main part to Harriet."

"She won't because she told me expressly that she feels Harriet isn't right for any of the main roles. She feels that Harriet has the star power to attract a lot of attention to the show, but artistically speaking, she doesn't feel Harriet is quite ready to carry the show all by herself since her voice simply isn't what she's looking for."

Well, she probably had a point, I thought. Harriet's voice may have power, but she lacks finesse, and these shows are probably about both. But since I had neither, Harriet had nothing to worry about. I wasn't going to get picked for any part, and I certainly wasn't going to audition either, and neither was Dooley. So I guess that was all for the good.

We had arrived at the cabin where Scarlett's captain was staying, and Chase pounded on the door with his fist. Judging from the look on his face and his stance, he wouldn't have minded putting one of those police battering rams to the door to force his way in. But then he wasn't in New York City, where that sort of thing is probably the customary way to visit any person you want to call on. Instead, he more or less politely knocked and bellowed, "Police, open up, Mr. Harper!"

Mr. Harper didn't open up, though, and when Chase expressed a concern that the man might have absconded through some other exit, Odelia assured him that there was simply no way, since these cabins don't have another exit. And no, the porthole didn't count, unless the man was suicidal.

Since patience has never been Chase's strong suit, moments later he put his shoulder to the door and gave it a gentle nudge. Though when I say gentle, I'm probably understating things. The door wasn't made to sustain such an assault and soon buckled under the pressure. It swung open, and Chase stormed in, only to come out again empty-handed. "Nothing," he said.

We entered, feeling more relaxed now that we knew this possible killer had left the premises, and inspected the room. Before long, we had ascertained that there was no trace of Maude's urn of ashes and also no trace of the loot the man had possibly stolen. No wallets or phones or anything that suggested that Scarlett and Gran's make-believe captain was also the real Captain Invisible.

"Too bad," said Chase as he surveyed the damage he'd inflicted on the door. "Looks like he's not our guy."

"But then why did he practically run away from Scarlett

when she mentioned that you're a cop and also Uncle Alec?" asked Odelia.

"Some people simply get nervous around cops," said Chase with a shrug. "That doesn't mean they did something wrong."

And with these words, we left the cabin, or we would have done so if not for the sudden appearance of a face in the door, taking one look at our company and breaking into a run.

"Hey, come back here!" Chase yelled and set off in pursuit of the guy, who I assumed just might be Jack Harper. Before long, we were all chasing after Chase, who was chasing after Mr. Harper. The chase could have taken us past scenic views such as the sun setting in the west or the stage being set for Mamma Mia, or people gathering on deck to do a bit of stargazing. It might even have taken us past the mini-golf course, always a popular pastime for many passengers. But instead, it ended abruptly when a hapless passenger happened to open his door. The door sustained a direct hit from Jack Harper, who found he lacked the brakes to halt his progress at such short notice, and smashed into the hapless passenger, who got squished between the door and the door jamb. Moments later, Chase was upon Mr. Harper, grabbed the man by the collar, and hoisted him up from the floor in one fluid motion, then pinned him up against the wall, his feet dangling two feet above the floor.

"You killed Maude Davis, didn't you, Jack? Confess!"

"What? Are you nuts?" the man squeaked. The squeaking was probably caused by the fact that Chase was applying undue pressure on the man's throat, causing his windpipe to protest in dismay. "I didn't kill anybody, man."

"Then why did you run?!" Chase thundered.

"Because I knew this was gonna happen, all right? Every time I run into one of you lot, I end up getting beaten up, knocked down, and generally end up in a worse way than I was before!"

"An innocent man doesn't run," Chase pointed out. "So let's try this again. Why did you run, Jack? And don't give me this crap about cops being all over you. They wouldn't be all over you if you didn't give them a good reason."

"Can you…" He gestured to his throat. "Please?"

Chase decided to ease up on the pressure and let the man down. Behind us, the passenger who had taken a hit from the door was moaning softly, and when Odelia took a closer look at the guy, she gasped in shock.

"It's Doctor Pearce!"

Only, of course, it wasn't. Not really. Since 'Doctor Pearce' didn't exist.

We all gathered around the remains of the man who had pretended to be a vet and said he was going to operate on my nose for my nonexistent skin tumor. His own nose wasn't much to look at the moment, since apparently it had received a direct hit from the door.

"He looks different," I said.

"He looks smushed," Dooley decided. "Smushed and soiled."

The soiled part probably referred to the tray of food he had been carrying, the contents of which had been transferred to his shirtfront. And his nose was a little battered from the hit he'd sustained.

"No, but his face is different. And also his hair."

And it was. He'd done something to his face that made it look narrower somehow. Possibly he'd used false teeth before and also some kind of fillers. And a wig, of course. We still recognized him, though, mainly because the man had given us such a big fright with his cancer prognosis.

From inside the room, the sound of a shower being turned off now sounded, and as a voice called out happily,

"Are you ready for some ABBA, Amos?" we all shared a look of surprise. The voice had sounded familiar. Could it be...

Moments later, a woman walked out of the bathroom. She stared at us, and we all stared back at her. Then Odelia said, "Madeline? What are you doing here?"

"Odelia?" Then she saw the remnants of the ex-vet and brought a distraught hand to her face. "Amos! What happened!"

"The ex-vet had a run-in with the door," Dooley said. "And the door had a run-in with the ex-captain. Or is it the other way around?"

"Yeah, I think the ex-captain had a run-in with the door," I said.

"Is he... your husband?" asked Odelia.

"Well, no," she admitted. "But he is my boyfriend. Not that it's any of your business."

"It kind of is my business," Odelia said, "because this is the guy who burgled our safe and stole our money, our passports, and our credit cards."

"What? But that's impossible!" said the captain, who was looking very un-captain-like in that towel wrapped around her person, with another towel wrapped around her head.

"I'm afraid so," said Odelia. "He's the guy pretending to be a vet, and then later he returned to burgle the safe. And it wouldn't surprise me if he isn't also the guy who stole from my grandmother and her friend." She gestured to the moaning man. "Captain Murray, meet Captain Invisible."

Chase, who was still holding onto Jack Harper, now hoisted the man into view. "You wouldn't by any chance be familiar with this guy, would you?"

Madeline stared at Jack Harper. "Mr. Harper," she said. "What happened to you?"

"The same thing that happened to your boyfriend," said Chase. "He hit the door from a north-eastern direction while this crook hit the door from a south-western direction. A neat case of two evils canceling each other out. Good riddance in both cases, I'd say."

"Amos doesn't have an evil bone in his body," said Madeline, and her cheeks colored. "And I would know."

"Okay, so I'm arresting this guy here for robbery," said Chase, stirring Captain Invisible with his foot. "And this guy for murder. And frankly speaking, I'm not sure why I wouldn't arrest you too, Madeline Murray, cause I have the distinct impression you're a little too familiar with these crooks!"

Madeline held up her hands now, then quickly returned them to her towel, lest it dropped to the floor and stopped protecting her modesty. "I can explain," she said. "Jack Harper is a fugitive from justice. Well, not really justice, more like a miscarriage of justice. When I met him this morning, he explained all of it to me when I revealed to him I was the captain. Apparently, his wife is suing him for assault and battery, even though he's innocent. She's been having an affair with a well-known media tycoon, and on his instigation, she figured she would get their divorce through a lot quicker, and also get custody of their kids, if she accused him of these heinous things, hoping the judge would side with her. And since her new boyfriend is not only rich but has access to top lawyers, Jack is almost certain to lose. If they can find him and subpoena him, which is why he's been hiding on cruise ships all this time. If his wife can't serve him with the papers, the divorce can't go through."

"That doesn't sound like a winning strategy," Chase grunted as he eyed the man with malice. Clearly, he wasn't buying it.

"Which is exactly what I told him. He should also lawyer up and fight his ex-wife on the charges she's bringing against him. All he needs is a couple of witnesses who can tell the judge his side of the story, and I'm sure he stands a very good chance at winning."

"I know I should probably go home and fight Allison," said Jack, looking like the broken wreckage of human remains he essentially was. His pride had obviously been broken, and if his face was any indication, now his nose had also suffered the same fate. "But I can't bring myself to face her, you know? Her future husband is this ultra-rich uberpowerful media guy who's got the best lawyers in his pocket, and maybe even the judge. So what chance do I stand? None."

"You have to think about your kids, Jack," said Madeline. "You're not just fighting for yourself and your reputation, you're also fighting for them. Or do you really want to see this other guy raise your kids?"

Jack winced and touched his nose. "I know you're right," he said quietly. "But I lack the stomach to do something about it."

"Like I told you this morning, contact my lawyer friend. She'll make sure you get a fair shake."

"So... this guy isn't Maude Davis's killer?" asked Chase, holding up the wreckage.

"No, he isn't," said Madeline.

"But this guy is a crook," said Odelia, referring to the man at her feet.

"Darn," said Madeline. "And I was just starting to like him. He's so charming, you wouldn't believe."

"He's also the guy your cruise line company has been looking for," said Chase. "So looks like he fooled you, Madeline, and he fooled you good."

The captain's cheeks flamed again, only this time it wasn't from embarrassment but from righteous anger for being hoodwinked by Amos.

"Okay, so what are the chances that Amos is Maude's killer?" asked Chase.

Odelia offered Madeline a radiant smile. "Would you mind very much if we searched the cabin?"

"Be my guest," said Madeline. "God, I can't believe I've been so stupid. The guy was probably laughing his ass off. Stealing from my passengers on the one hand and dating me on the other. What a piece of work."

It didn't take long for Odelia to discover the man's hidden stash. At the back of one of the closets, a large cardboard box sat, and when she opened it, it was like discovering Aladdin's cave. Well, maybe not really, but it was still a nice haul. Inside the box she found phones, wallets, envelopes filled with cash, jewelry, Rolexes and other expensive watches... She also found her own wallet and Chase's, and also Gran and Scarlett's. "Looks like Captain Invisible is invisible no more," she said.

The thief had come to, and as he opened his eyes and rubbed his head, he seemed surprised to find himself surrounded by a group of people looking at him with distinct interest. "What happened?" he asked.

"You got busted, buddy," said Chase. Odelia held up the box, and the guy closed his eyes again and groaned.

"How could you!" Madeline shouted.

He shrugged. "How could I not? You're a remarkable woman, Maddie, although when I tell you that I've fallen in love with you, you probably won't believe me."

"No, I won't," said Madeline. She stared daggers at the man, then said, "You're under arrest and will be confined to the brig until we can hand you over to the proper authorities."

"You're making a big mistake, Maddie."

"Oh, stop calling me that."

"You love me, you know you do."

"Is Amos even your real name?"

He hesitated, and it was clear that he'd lied about that as well.

"Oliver Pearce is what he called himself," said Odelia.

"So what is your real name?" asked Chase. But when the guy shrugged, he added, "Don't worry. We'll figure it out... Captain Invisible."

The fake vet winced. "Oh, rats," he muttered.

# CHAPTER 19

Mamma Mia had been a huge success, or at least according to Marge and Tex, who had enjoyed it tremendously. Uncle Alec said he had fallen asleep midway through the show, and Charlene said it wasn't bad, but she preferred the movie. And Gran and Scarlett had skipped the show and had watched the stars on deck instead. They had talked a lot about life and their friendship and seemed to have resolved their differences.

"Odd how a man can split friends apart," said Dooley. "But also how the wrong man can bring them back together again."

It wasn't a given that Jack Harper was a 'wrong man' though. Apparently, he was a good man who had gone into hiding from his soon-to-be ex-wife. But as Madeline had given him another pep talk, he promised to man up and face the firing squad in the form of the battery of expensive lawyers his wife had lined up. It wouldn't be easy, but for his own sake and that of his kids, he was prepared to go into battle.

The fake vet who had diagnosed me with a fatal disease

was safely locked away in the brig, and his loot had been returned to the people he had stolen it from. Madeline would be fine. The only thing she had lost was her innocence. Or at least that's how Dooley put it. I wasn't sure he was correct in this determination, but she certainly had lost a few of her illusions.

The only case we hadn't solved yet was that of Maude Davis, but since we were arriving at our next port soon, and the FBI had already been in contact with Madeline about the case, they would take over and relieve us of our investigative duties. In a sense, it was a pity since I don't like to walk away from a case, but then we weren't really involved in an official capacity, per se, since we were on vacation. And since Marge and Tex were the celebrated couple, they were probably relieved that the investigation was at an end.

Which is why it came as something of a surprise when a letter arrived the next morning. It had been slipped underneath the door of our cabin and contained the following message:

*To Whom It May Concern:*

*Circus Bodoni was a mainstay in the lives of many people over the years. In the forty years the circus was in existence, it enriched the lives of both its artists but also of the people who visited the circus and awarded the troupe its patronage. And many of them stayed loyal to the circus until the very end. But when the economy made things impossible to continue, and Clark Davis was forced to close down the circus, one man felt so betrayed he swore a solemn oath not to rest until he had destroyed the person he held responsible for the breaking up of the only family he ever had. This person worked for the circus as a juggler for many years and never knew anything else since he had been introduced into the profession at the age of ten when his parents had deserted him, and Clark and*

NIC SAINT

*Maude Davis took him under their wing. So when the circus folded, it hit him harder than most. And what's more, he blamed both Clark and Maude for not doing what was necessary to keep going. If they had wanted to, they could have kept the circus alive, but apparently Clark preferred the money he could get from selling the circus's assets to safeguarding the troupe's survival.*

*And so the plan started to crystalize that Clark had to pay the ultimate price for his betrayal. And when Clark died, shocking all those near and dear to him, the plan shifted, and this time the juggler took Maude into his sights. It seemed apt, for he firmly believed that it was, in fact, Maude who was to blame, even more than Clark himself. Clark Davis had proven a weak man, and under the influence of Maude, who wanted out of the hard life of a circus artist and to spend the money they had made over the years, he had decided to pull the plug.*

*The juggler was sure Maude was the evil genius behind the bankruptcy. He was also sure that Maude had killed her own husband. She hadn't just poisoned Clark's mind against the circus life, but she had also poisoned his body. If only the juggler could get his hands on the man's ashes, he could prove they probably contained plenty of arsenic. But that was the problem: Maude kept Clark's urn with her at all times. And for a good reason. She knew it contained incriminating material in the form of the poison she had used to murder her husband. So when the juggler learned she was taking one final cruise so she could scatter his ashes, he knew it was his only chance to prove once and for all that Maude was a murderer and to bring her to justice.*

*Only things didn't go exactly as I had planned...*

ODELIA FINISHED READING the letter and looked up into her husband's face. We had just woken up from a pleasant sleep, and frankly, my mind wasn't exactly buzzing along at full capacity yet, but it now seemed clear that Maude's death was connected to the circus she and her husband had run for many years.

"What do you think?" asked Odelia.

"I think that the killer wants us to inspect those ashes and determine whether Maude murdered her husband Clark or not," said Chase.

"So where are the ashes?" asked Odelia. She held up the letter. "It doesn't say anything about that."

"Maybe it's a riddle," Chase suggested. "And you're supposed to solve the riddle, and it will lead you to Clark Davis's urn?"

"It is possible," said Odelia, studying the letter once more. "I'm not very good at this sort of thing, though. Riddles and puzzles are not my strong suit."

"Maybe ask your dad," Chase suggested. "He's the only one in our family who manages to finish the *New York Times* crossword puzzle."

It was true. Tex loved the crossword puzzle and did it every Saturday. So if there really was a code to be cracked, maybe he could take a crack at it and solve it. And so the present company moved next door, where Tex and Marge had just finished taking a shower and were getting ready to head to breakfast. When his daughter handed him the letter, the doctor seemed properly intrigued. "I'll give it my best shot," he promised. "Though it doesn't look straightforward. First letter of each sentence doesn't yield anything, and neither does reversing the order of the words." He sank down on a chair and studied the letter with distinct interest.

Grace, who had been following the back and forth, now piped up, "Maybe you could check the letter for fingerprints?"

We relayed her words to Odelia, and Chase nodded. "Unfortunately, we don't have that capability here. But once the FBI comes on board, they can send it off to their lab for testing."

"The clue must be hidden in that letter," said Grace. "Not just the location of the urn but also the identity of Maude's killer. Obviously, this juggler didn't want to kill her. All he wanted was to expose her. And in the process, he ended up killing her, possibly because they got involved in a struggle over that urn. If Maude did indeed murder her husband, it stood to reason that she wouldn't want anyone to lay their hands on those ashes, so she would have fought the killer hard."

It was perfectly sound reasoning, and we all stared at the toddler with unveiled admiration. "Did you work all of that out by yourself?" asked Harriet.

Grace shrugged. "It wasn't hard. When you grow up in a family of sleuths, I guess it kinda rubs off on you after a while."

"Just don't go out there hunting clues all by yourself, you hear?" said Harriet sternly. "Playing detective isn't a kid's game. So don't try this out at home."

Grace grinned. "Thanks for the advice, Harriet. Though maybe you should take your own advice and not get involved either, for it's equally dangerous to cats, you know. You guys are even smaller than I am. If this killer wanted to, he could make mincemeat of you."

We all gulped a little at this very vivid word picture she had painted. "Max, I don't want to be turned into mincemeat!" said Dooley.

"Now look what you've done," said Harriet. "Now you have upset Dooley."

"I'm sorry, Dooley," said Grace. "Nobody is going to make mincemeat of you. Because no humans like to eat cat meat. They might put you in that urn, though."

"But... I don't fit inside an urn," said Dooley, much dismayed.

"Of course you don't, silly! First they'd have to kill you and turn you to ashes."

Dooley practically squealed, "But I don't want to be turned into ashes!"

"Grace!" said Harriet. "Stop scaring Dooley."

"Oh, all right," said Grace with an eye roll. "You guys can't take a joke, can you?" She toddled over to Dooley and gently stroked his fur. "I'm sorry, Dooley. I didn't mean to upset you. I was only joking. Nobody is going to make mincemeat of you, and nobody is going to turn you into ashes."

"Are you sure?" asked Dooley.

"Absolutely. So don't you worry about a thing. And now," she said as she plopped herself down on the floor, "we have to figure out who this killer is and where he has hidden Clark's urn."

I would have handed her that letter, but unfortunately, Grace couldn't read yet. But as the toddler gave the mystery of the letter some more thought, she said something that struck a chord with me.

"No matter how fast you run," she said, "you can never outrun your past, can you?"

Which is what sparked an idea in me. An idea I decided to give a little more thought, for it just might be important. It didn't take me long to formulate a theory, and when I told Odelia, and she told Chase, the cop decided to put my theory to the test. When moments later he called to say that Maude's body had disappeared from the freezer, it became obvious that my hunch was correct.

## CHAPTER 20

*It* was a sunny day when the Ruritania arrived at Boris Island. A line of passengers had already formed, eager to go ashore and frequent the pleasant little craft shops the island boasted, the restaurants offering typical local dishes, and generally enjoy being off the ship for a couple of hours. Not all passengers liked to leave the ship, though, to join the shore excursions and tours. Some preferred to stay on board for the duration of their journey and spend time lounging by the pool.

But as the line progressed and passenger after passenger walked the ramp down to the quay, they noticed a strange scene. A small group of people seemed to scan their faces, one after the other, almost as if they were looking for someone. The group consisted of Captain Madeline Murray, head of security Claude Monier, a blond-haired woman, and a powerfully built young man. And strangely: four cats accompanied the group. Now, that was probably the oddest part of all.

* * *

"Are you sure about this, Kingsley?" asked Claude for the umpteenth time.

"Yes, Monier," said Chase. "Absolutely."

"Because if you're wrong, there will be hell to pay. Not to mention we will both become the laughingstock of the FBI, who have just messaged me that they're ready to board the ship the moment these passengers have finished going ashore."

"Let's put a little faith in Detective Kingsley, Claude," the captain suggested. "I think his reasoning is very sound, especially after we discovered that Maude Davis's body has gone missing from the morgue, and also the statement we just took from Mr. Morgan."

"What statement? Henry Morgan is a raging alcoholic," Claude scoffed. "I wouldn't believe anything that comes out of that man's mouth."

"And yet he heard what he heard," Odelia pointed out.

After I had my brainwave, brought on by what Grace said, it didn't take me long to figure out that someone must have witnessed that body going overboard. Bodies don't simply disappear, so someone must have dumped it overboard. Before long Chase and Odelia had hit upon a witness. CCTV footage had already ascertained that the person who made Maude's body disappear knew exactly where the cameras were hidden and had avoided being filmed. But they hadn't counted on Henry Morgan having once again fallen off the wagon, at which point he had decided to take a stroll on deck to sober up. He had a Skype call coming up with his daughters, and he definitely didn't want them to see him in that state. And so when he was walking the deck that night and had heard a splash, he had gone looking for the source of the sound, worried that someone may have gone overboard. What he hadn't counted on was that he would come face to face with Maude's killer.

The description he had given us was the final push Chase needed to give credence to my theory. And so he told Madeline, who had organized this little mission.

"Are you sure, Max?" Odelia now whispered. "We've almost run out of passengers!"

She was right. Most of the passengers had already disembarked, with only a few stragglers waiting in line. And that's when I saw the man. He was big with a round face, a big nose, and a big belly, just as Frank the sausage dog had told us.

"That's him!" I shouted immediately. "That's the killer!"

Immediately, Claude and his team sprang into action. And as the killer realized he had been spotted, he tried to run back but soon found that another guard was waiting behind him, ready to catch him if he ran. And so he did the only thing possible: he jumped into the water! There was only a narrow strip between the ship and the quay, so this initiative was fraught with a lot of danger.

"He's getting away!" Claude shouted.

But he shouldn't have worried. As the killer swam to shore, he was greeted by a small posse of FBI agents who were only too eager to help him ashore before slapping a pair of handcuffs on his wrists. And as we all hurried down the ramp to join them, we saw that the man's face had become bloated, and also that his nose had suddenly gone crooked. It didn't take the FBI agents long to determine that the killer was wearing a mask.

They stripped it off, and the face of a woman appeared.

"Who's this?!" Claude yelled, grabbing his hair in dismay.

"This," I said, "is Maude Davis."

After Odelia had relayed my words to the others, they all stared at the woman. She didn't look the least bit defiant. If anything, she looked completely undone. She was crying buckets of tears and generally looked as if she was on the verge of collapsing into a heap. And of course, she had every reason to, for being arrested meant she would have to face charges. And that also meant she would probably be extradited back to the States to face those charges. At which point this whole charade she had set up would all have been for naught.

Harriet turned to me. "Max," she said. "I don't understand anything!"

"Me neither," Brutus confessed.

"I think she's the zombie queen," said Dooley, nodding seriously. "The dog snatcher Max was talking about." He gave me a look of admiration. "You were right all along, Max. She's real!"

# EPILOGUE

*O*nce again, we were on deck, only this time we were watching Chase practice some smooth moves on the surf simulator. It was like a big pool with artificially created waves that mimicked the sensation of riding actual waves. And since Chase had been eager to give the thing a try, he was having a ball now, even though he kept falling off his surfboard at regular intervals. But then that's all part and parcel of learning a new discipline. Every time he fell off his board, Marge, Odelia, Gran, and Charlene winced, and so did Grace. Tex and Uncle Alec seemed less concerned with the fate of their friend and relative. They probably figured Chase was a big boy and could take a hit.

Next to me, Harriet and Brutus had stretched out, and so had Dooley. And as I told the story of how we had caught Maude Davis's killer, who turned out to be Maude Davis herself, they paid more attention to me than to Chase's acrobatics. I guess cats aren't all that worried when humans do stupid stunts. Okay, so we scratch our heads and wonder why. Why do people want to climb to the top of a particular mountain? Why do they want to travel to the North Pole?

And why do they want to use a flimsy fiberglass and polyester board to brave a crushing wave? Because they're nuts, that's why. But as long as they don't drag us into the fray, it's all fine.

"Okay, so Maude isn't dead?" asked Dooley.

"No, Maude isn't dead, Dooley," I said. "In fact she's very much alive."

"But we saw her body. She was lying on her bed in her cabin—dead."

"That wasn't Maude. That was an unfortunate woman Maude met at the last port we visited before Boris Island. Maude had gone on a shore excursion and met Lily Doyle, a talented artist who owned an art gallery in town. She bought a ton of paintings from the owner, and convinced her to help bring them to her cabin. That's when she murdered the woman."

"But why, Max? Why?"

"Because she looked like her, right?" asked Harriet. "Even you thought she was Maude Davis."

"There was a remarkable resemblance," I agreed. "Which was the impetus that made her decide on this course of action. You see, Maude had been thinking about disappearing from her own life for a while. Ever since Circus Bodoni failed, in fact. More than a fair few of the circus artists were very unhappy with the Davises after that. They blamed Clark but also Maude for this blow to their livelihoods. Many of them had been with the circus for many years, some since they were kids."

"Like the juggler who wrote that letter?" asked Harriet.

"Maude wrote that letter," I said. "And slipped it underneath the door of our cabin. She wanted to point the blame for her murder to the juggler, whose actual name was Robert Hill."

"So this Robert Hill didn't write the letter?"

"No, he didn't, because Mr. Hill is dead. Maude killed him before she embarked on this trip. It was part of her plan to disappear. You see, Robert Hill was the main spokesperson for the group that wanted to sue Clark and Maude for the bankruptcy of Circus Bodoni. They claimed that the circus should never have defaulted. That there was plenty of money left to keep operating. But that Clark had put the money in his pocket and caused the circus to collapse under the mountain of debt he had artificially created. He then set up his zoo and animal training business with the money but still had plenty squirreled away so he and Maude could live well for the rest of their lives. Only fate decided differently. Clark didn't get to enjoy his riches very long, for he got sick and died. And then Robert started accusing Maude of poisoning her husband so she could lay her hands on the money."

"Do you think Maude poisoned Clark, Max?" asked Dooley.

"Yes, she did," I said. "And then she disposed of his ashes by dumping them into the ocean, probably the moment the ship left home port."

"Even though she told Henry that the urn was still in her room?" asked Harriet.

"Absolutely. She was setting up her cover story, you see. The thing was that Robert Hill was making things really difficult for her, the same way he had made things difficult for Clark before. He simply wouldn't let go and had really dug his teeth in and was making a lot of waves."

"So she killed him," said Harriet.

"Yes, she did. And fed his body to her lions. And then she set out on this cruise, determined to disappear for good and escape from all the Robert Hills of this world and all of her other critics, and enjoy her money in a non-extradition country where she would live under an assumed name. Her original plan was to simply disappear and make people believe she had fallen overboard. But then when she met Lily Doyle in that gallery on Valley Island, and noticed the striking resemblance, a different plan occurred to her. She would murder this woman artist and make it look as if she had died at Robert Hill's hands. And since the police and the rest of the world would think that Maude was dead, and that Robert Hill had killed her, that would be the end of that part of her life."

"Is that why she dumped the body of that other woman overboard?"

"She needed to get rid of the body before the FBI boarded the boat. Before they could discover that it wasn't Maude lying in the morgue but Lily Doyle, owner of an art gallery on Valley Island."

After Maude's arrest, the FBI had interrogated her, and she had confessed everything. She had also given them the name of the woman she had been passing off as herself. Mrs. Doyle's body probably would never be recovered, as it had been swept away, but at least they could give her family peace of mind since they had been worried sick after her sudden disappearance from her gallery that afternoon after Maude's big purchase. Maude had confessed to murdering the woman and also murdering her husband Clark and Robert Hill, which made her a triple murderer.

"Good thing Henry Morgan never went back with her that night," said Brutus. "Or he might have ended up dead as well."

"I think that was all part of the charade," I said. "She wanted someone to testify that she was alive at that moment, and then she made a lot of noise when she was supposedly being murdered, to make sure we would think she had died at two o'clock, when in actual fact she had murdered Mrs. Doyle the day before, after the Ruritania had visited Valley Island. It was all part of the stage play she was setting up, and both Henry Morgan and David Adams were key witnesses."

"And suspects," Brutus added.

"Yeah, that was a nice bonus, since it would send the police running around in circles until the letter arrived that would point the finger at Robert Hill instead. And then by the time her body was discovered missing, we would all believe that Mr. Hill had pulled off the perfect murder."

"When in actual fact, the poor man was dead all along."

"It was a nice set-up," said Harriet. "But in the end, it failed."

"So how did you figure it out, Max?" asked Brutus.

"Something Grace said."

Grace, who was seated next to us and who had been covering her eyes so she wouldn't have to watch her dad suffer wipeout after wipeout, now glanced at me. "I solved the murder?"

"Pretty much," I said with a smile. "When that letter arrived, you said we can't outrun our past."

"Which is a pretty deep statement," said Harriet as she gave Grace a nudge.

"Of course," said Grace. "That's because I am a very deep person."

"That, you are," said Harriet, laughing.

"So that got me thinking. Obviously, Maude was being accused of murdering her husband in that letter. So what if she had? And what if she was trying to get rid of her old life and start a new one? How would she have to go about that? Also, I remembered those paintings Odelia discovered underneath her bed. They didn't seem to fit in with the other stuff Maude had picked up during her shore excursions. Those paintings were professionally made, all by the same artist, while the rest was cheap bric-a-brac stuff you can pick up at any store catering to tourists."

"She probably should have gotten rid of those paintings," said Harriet.

"Yeah, but she couldn't find it in her heart to destroy them," said Brutus.

"I think you're taking a too charitable view," I said. "I think she was going to destroy them but simply forgot or ran out of time."

We were silent for a moment, then Dooley said, "I guess it's not easy to organize your own murder, especially on such short notice. That's a lot of moving parts, Max. I'm not sure I could do it." He gave me a sideways glance. "I'm sure you could, though. Your brain is big enough to pull it off."

Brutus grinned at this. "Max could probably get away with murder. So how about it, buddy? Who do you want to kill?"

I gave him a stern-faced look. "Murder is nothing to make jokes about, Brutus."

"All right, all right," he said, holding up his paws.

"Max is right," said Harriet. "Lily Doyle's family aren't laughing right now."

"At least they'll get her paintings back," said Dooley. "And if they keep looking, maybe her body. Unless that big squid that's been following the Ruritania hasn't eaten her, or that shoal of sharks."

Something told me Lily's body probably wouldn't be found. Which had all been part of Maude's plan. No body, no Maude. She would have died, and that would have been the end of that. She would have stepped ashore on Boris Island and vanished into thin air, assuming a new identity and living the life of a wealthy widow.

Grace winced as her daddy suffered another wipeout. He seemed to have had enough, though, for he now crawled out of the pool and toweled himself off before joining the rest of the family.

"Now it's your turn, buddy," he told Uncle Alec.

"Never!" said the Chief.

"Yeah, over my dead body," Charlene quipped. "I want to marry a living, breathing person, not a dead one."

"Oh, it won't kill you," said Chase. "In fact, it might do you some good. It's exhilarating!"

"So exhilarating I couldn't even watch," said Marge.

"Good thing there's a doctor present," Tex quipped.

"And a loving wife who will nurse you back to health!" Odelia added.

"Why, oh why are grown-ups so dumb, Max?" asked Grace. "To risk their lives by crawling into that horrible simulator and step on that surfboard?"

"Now that," I told her, "is a mystery I haven't been able to solve yet."

"But we're working on it," Dooley added for her benefit.

Grace laughed at this. "At least you guys are normal. If I didn't have you, what kind of role models would I have?" She glanced at her dad who was sparring with Uncle Alec, landing gentle jabs on the man's chest, Gran and Scarlett who were arguing about who was going to marry Jack Harper once his divorce finally came through, Charlene, who was asking Odelia for advice about getting pregnant at fifty, and Marge and Tex discussing the pros and cons of swimming with sharks.

"It's supposed to be very safe," Tex was saying. "Safer than swimming with dolphins, even."

"Apart from you guys, at least one person in this family has some sense," Grace said and snuggled up to her grandmother, pleasantly surprising Marge.

And as my eyes drooped closed, I wondered not for the first time how often we would get the chance to enjoy each other's company like this. As far as I was concerned: not nearly often enough. Which is why I was determined to enjoy every minute of it. But first, I needed a nice long nap to recharge that big brain of mine, as Dooley likes to put it. Some people claim that brains operate on sugar. I guess I'm the exception to the rule, for my brain works purely on naps. And I need lots of them!

"Max?"

"Mh?"

"Are you asleep?"

"I was asleep, Dooley."

"So now that our cruise trip has been comped, does that mean we have to come out here again next year and do this all over again?"

"I guess so," I said. "But hopefully without the dead bodies this time."

"Oh, Max," he said with a chuckle. "The day we can get through a vacation without stumbling over dead bodies is the day motels freeze over."

"I think it's hell that freezes over," I said.

"Is it? That would probably make a lot more sense."

At which point he snuggled up to me, and we fell asleep together.

## THE END

**Thanks for reading! If you want to know when a new Nic Saint book comes out, sign up for Nic's mailing list: nicsaint.com/news**

# EXCERPT FROM PURRFECT ZOO (MAX 69)

**Chapter One**

Robert Ross looked down at the dog he was walking and wondered if he'd ever seen a finer specimen of the canine species. Marlin was perfectly proportioned, with the perfect type of fur, the perfect tawny color, and from the way he looked up at him, you could see that he was without a doubt the most intelligent dog that had ever lived. His gaze exuded smarts and just a hint of arrogance, which actually suited him well. Marlin had been his trusty canine companion for going on three years now, and Robert wouldn't have wanted it any other way. If he'd listened to Kimberly back when they'd first dropped by the pound to look at prospective candidates to fill the rather large shoes Marlin's predecessor Franklin had left, they would have taken a Chihuahua. "It fits so nicely on your lap," she had said. "And we can take it anywhere with us, even when we're traveling by plane."

But Robert had wandered off to look at some of the other canines while Kimberly stuck with the Chihuahua, asking the pound owner about a million questions. That's when he spotted Marlin, tucked away at the back of his cage, looking sad and forlorn. He didn't even respond when Robert crouched down in front of his cage and tried to engage the creature in conversation. Clearly, something traumatic had happened to the dog, and he had become locked in his own shell, retreating from the world.

For some reason, the dog had appealed to him in a big way, so he'd interrupted his wife's harangue and asked the pound owner about Marlin's history. It was the typical litany of being shifted from one owner to the next until the dog's proud spirit had been broken, and he had given up hope and belief that he'd ever find a true forever home.

That's when Robert decided to do just that. And so he'd taken Marlin home—funny name for a dog, but the pound owner didn't think it was wise to change his name now, since he was already used to it—against Kimberly's protestations, and he hadn't regretted it a single day.

It had taken a while for them to gain Marlin's trust, as the dog hadn't believed this could be it. That these people wouldn't return him to the pound after a couple of days, with a nasty case of buyer's remorse, but eventually he'd started to relax and become accustomed to his new home and his new humans. Pretty soon, Marlin and Robert had become inseparable, with Kimberly complaining that he seemed to like the damn dog more than her. But then Marlin was so loyal, so loving, and so giving it wasn't any wonder that Robert adored the creature, and in due course, the dog had also become fond of him, the man who had saved him from that dreadful fate back at the pound.

The dog barked once, and Robert knew exactly what that meant. He was ready to go to the dog park, to do his business but also to play with the other dogs while Robert chatted with the other dog owners.

And as they set foot and paw to the dog park, Robert

thought not for the first time that he may have saved the dog, but the dog had also saved him.

The dog park was pretty busy at this time of the morning, but he didn't mind. He knew most of the other people there, and by now Marlin knew most of the other dogs and got along with them very well indeed.

Robert let Marlin off his leash, and immediately the dog made a beeline for a small group of fellow canines. They were a big sheepdog answering to the name Rufus and a small Yorkie answering to the name Fifi, and he got along with those two particularly well for some reason.

Robert walked over to the dogs' respective owners: Ted Trapper and Kurt Mayfield, and the men greeted him with a curt nod of the head.

"Marlin is looking good today," said Ted, the most talkative of the duo.

"Yeah, he's been feeling good," he said with satisfaction. "I gave him some extra-juicy leftovers this morning, and he seemed to like it. He's had some tummy trouble the last couple of days, and the vet said we shouldn't feed him kibble for a while, only food straight from our table, and see if it makes a difference."

"If I gave Fifi food straight from the table," grunted Kurt Mayfield, "she'd be hopping all over our table all the time." He grinned. "I wouldn't mind, though. Once you've got a dog, there's nothing you wouldn't do for the furry creature, is there?"

"Yeah, isn't that just the case?" said Ted with a happy sigh. "Though I gotta admit, Marcie doesn't always feel the same way."

"Yeah, my girlfriend doesn't either," Kurt confessed. "She likes Fifi and tolerates her to some extent for my sake, but if she's totally honest, I think she wouldn't mind if she wasn't there."

## EXCERPT FROM PURRFECT ZOO (MAX 69)

"My wife had her doubts about Marlin," said Robert. "When we picked him up at the pound, she actually wanted to adopt a Chihuahua, but I managed to talk her into adopting Marlin instead. I mean, Chihuahuas are popular, and that dog would have been adopted by anyone, but Marlin was one of those rejects that nobody seemed to want. He kept being shifted back to the pound by the respective adoptive parents that took him in until he was so demoralized he just retreated into a world of his own. You should have seen him when I first laid eyes on him."

"And look at him now," said Kurt. "The happiest and liveliest dog in the dog park."

Robert watched as Marlin, Fifi, and Rufus played happily together, not a care in the world, and felt gratified once again that he had followed his intuition and decided to take a chance on the mutt. It was only fair since Marlin had to take a chance on his new pet parents. And it had worked out to their satisfaction — both human and dog.

He looked up where a sort of commotion alerted them that something was going down on the street side of the dog park.

"Who's that?" asked Robert, referring to an older lady who was passing by in the company of no less than four cats.

"Oh, that's Vesta Muffin," said Kurt. "She's my neighbor."

"Yeah, my next-door neighbor too," said Ted. "She's crazy but also nice."

"That describes her to a T," said Kurt with a grin. "The whole family is nice but crazy. And I've had to endure the presence of those four cats for a while now, and I gotta say, it hasn't always been easy. They have this habit of caterwauling in the middle of the night for some reason, and when I say something about it, Vesta gets upset, and so does the rest of the family."

"Crazy cat family, huh?" said Robert. He didn't mind. He

### EXCERPT FROM PURRFECT ZOO (MAX 69)

was crazy about Marlin, so he could understand that there were folks out there who were crazy about their cats. To each their own.

"The daughter works at the library," Kurt continued, "and is married to a doctor. Then there's the granddaughter who's a reporter and sometime amateur detective. She's married to a cop. And there's also a great-granddaughter who likes to toddle around the backyard and play with the cats."

Robert winced. "Isn't that awfully dangerous? I mean, cats and toddlers, that can't be a great combination, right?"

"Oh, no, it's fine," Ted assured him. "They're very well-behaved, those Poole cats. In fact..." He glanced over at Kurt, then quickly closed his mouth, as if he'd said something wrong.

"In fact, what?" asked Robert.

"Nothing," Ted said. "Oh, will you look at that? Our dogs and Vesta's cats are hanging out together. Isn't that cute?"

Robert eyed the strange scene with interest. It was true: their dogs and that old lady's cats did indeed seem to enjoy spending time together, which was unusual, he thought, since cats and dogs don't always get along.

"It's almost as if they're... talking to each other," he said.

Kurt and Ted shared another look, and he had a feeling there was something they weren't telling him.

"What?" he asked then. "What is it?"

Kurt shrugged. "It's just a rumor, but..."

"I don't believe it myself, to be honest," said Ted.

"Me neither," Kurt assured them.

"What rumor? What are you talking about?"

"Well, rumor has it that the three ladies—grandmother, daughter, and granddaughter—are able to communicate with their cats."

Robert waited for the punchline, but when it didn't come and the two men remained serious, he frowned. "But that's impossible. Humans can't communicate with cats, just like we can't communicate with dogs." Though wouldn't it be nice if he could? He sure would like to know what Marlin was thinking sometimes. And he wouldn't mind telling him what he was thinking.

"It's just a rumor," Ted said with a shrug. "I'm not sure if it's true."

"It can't be true," said Robert decidedly. "The laws of nature don't allow it. If all species had the ability to communicate with each other, that would mean we could talk to birds, to chickens, to... to ducks in the pond." He laughed. "It would be like living in a Disney movie!"

"Like Ted said," said Kurt. "It's just a crazy rumor. Frankly, I don't believe a word of it. Just gossip, you know. I mean, you know what people are like, especially in a small town like ours."

"Oh, I sure do," Robert said. He and Kimberly had only moved to Hampton Cove six months ago, and already Kimberly was regretting their decision, complaining that Hampton Cove was like a dead zone where nothing ever happened, and where the people weren't friendly to her. She claimed that when she went shopping, they simply ignored her, then started gossiping about her behind her back. Robert had suggested she join some clubs, but Kimberly said there weren't any, which he found hard to believe, since every town has clubs.

At least they had their jobs, which guaranteed some human interaction with their colleagues. And of course, there were Ted and Kurt at the dog park. Those guys had taken him in from the beginning and hadn't even looked down their noses at him even once. That was the beauty of being a dog owner: whether you lived in Hampton Cove, Albuquerque, or the moon, you always had something in common. Like a secret club you were all members of.

The cats seemed to have moved on, and the old lady disappeared around the corner. It seemed a little weird to Robert that she would be walking her cats, just like the rest of them walked their dogs, but then she probably was a little eccentric, if those rumors were circling around that she could talk to her cats. Maybe she did talk to her cats, and maybe she even believed that her cats talked back to her. But all in all, it was nonsense, of course, and the woman probably had a screw loose.

**Chapter Two**

"So who's the new guy talking to Ted and Kurt?" asked Brutus.

"Um... I think his name is Robert," said Gran. "He moved into the old Michaelson place down the street. That house that was totally run down? They've fixed it up nice, and now it's a real credit to the neighborhood. I haven't actually met them yet, but talk around the block is that the woman is really snooty. The guy is all right. Friendly with all the neighbors."

"He sure seemed friendly with Ted and Kurt," said Brutus. "But then he probably has to be if he wants to become part of our local community."

"It's not easy," said Gran. "Some of our neighbors aren't always as welcoming as they could be. They don't like newcomers, especially when they're not from around these parts and if they haven't lived here for at least ten generations."

Brutus laughed. "Ten generations!"

"Have you lived here ten generations, Gran?" asked Dooley.

Gran nodded. "I guess so. I've never actually tracked my pedigree, you know, but it wouldn't surprise me if my forebears arrived here many years ago and helped put this town on the map." She frowned. "I just hope that the Rosses will start to feel at home here. A community needs fresh blood. And I have to say, Ted and Kurt have some great things to say about Robert and Kimberly Ross. They're both schoolteachers, and by all accounts, they're both real popular with their students."

"Snooty or not, that's nice," said Max.

Vesta grinned at the big red cat. "Kids never think anyone is snooty, and I think that even if you are snooty, it's very difficult to be snooty with kids since they're so disarming and don't care what you wear or what you look like. They haven't been spoiled by the world yet."

"Like Grace?" asked Dooley.

Vesta nodded. "Yeah, exactly like Grace." She adored her great-granddaughter and thought she was just about the most gorgeous little treasure that had ever been put on this planet.

She quickly walked on, suddenly remembering the whole reason she had come out in the first place. "We better get a move on, you guys," she said, urging on her small clowder of cats. "We don't want to be late for our next visit."

She had been selected, along with a couple of other cat parents, to present an award to the best pet parent in Hampton Cove. It was a prestigious thing, and she was happy that they'd chosen her to give out the award, as organized by the Hampton Cove Pet Owners Society. All the pet parents in town were eligible to select candidates and award points. She would have selected her granddaughter, who she thought was simply wonderful with their cats, but that's not how the competition worked. You couldn't select members of your own family. Otherwise, everyone would do that, and nobody would get enough points to qualify for the big prize.

So over the course of the next couple of weeks, the

members of the jury, of which Vesta was a member, had to pay a visit to the different pet parents and monitor their activities, interview them about their habits and their everyday life, and generally decide how well they were treating their pets and how happy those pets were. At first, Vesta had balked at the whole idea of pitting pet parents against one another, figuring there was no need for such an award. But after having spoken to the organizing committee and especially the chair of that committee, Marjorie Sooms, she understood that there was a reason they had decided to organize the competition. There had been rumors about people neglecting their pets and not treating them as well as they should. So this whole award business was an opportunity for them to discreetly take a closer look at some of the dynamics at play between pet and pet parent and possibly offer suggestions on how to improve that relationship. And if they happened to come across a flagrant case of neglect or even outright abuse, they'd notify the proper authorities, and they could launch an official inquiry and even remove the pet from that home.

It was a noble cause, and so Vesta had wholeheartedly given it her support.

Which is why she was now on her way to talk to just such a family. And because she couldn't talk to dogs herself, she had decided to take one of her cats along, knowing that they could talk to dogs and would alert her if there was anything out of the ordinary. But since she couldn't just pick one cat, since the others would feel neglected or left out, she had to take all four of them. It was a strange sight, but then as the official representative of the Hampton Cove Pet Owners Society, it wasn't unheard of for her to be accompanied by her own pets. People might look at her a little strange, but by now most of them knew that she often ventured out with her

## EXCERPT FROM PURRFECT ZOO (MAX 69)

four fur-balls in tow, and so did her daughter and granddaughter.

They had arrived at their destination, and she applied her finger to the buzzer. When no response came, she glanced through the little window next to the door to see if she could spot the owner of the house.

"Strange," she said. "I confirmed our appointment last night."

"Maybe they're out back," Max said. "And can't hear the bell."

"I guess so," said Vesta. And since she didn't want to stand on that porch all day, she figured she might as well do a little harmless trespassing to see if Max's theory was correct.

The cats were already heading that way, and she followed. And it was when she arrived in the backyard that she saw it: the lady of the house was seated on the swing at the back of the garden, looking dead to the world. She smiled and headed over there. She knew that Chloe Fisher was a well-known interior designer, married to an ad exec, and they were the proud owners of a lovely little Bichon Frisé who answered to the name Bella. And it was Bella she now saw, seated at the feet of her mistress, and barking up a storm the moment they arrived on the scene. And she had just reached the duo when she saw, to her dismay, that Chloe still hadn't moved an inch. And as she reached out a hand to alert the woman of their presence, suddenly Chloe Fisher... dropped from the swing and fell to the floor.

Her eyes were open, but she was very obviously dead.

### Chapter Three

I don't know if you've ever seen a dead person, but if you haven't, I can't say I'd recommend the experience. It's a little disconcerting, to say the least, and even though I have

## EXCERPT FROM PURRFECT ZOO (MAX 69)

witnessed my fair share of the deceased, it never fails to give me the willies, to be honest. Especially as this particular person dropped right in front of me, causing me to gaze into her eyes for a moment before I finally managed to drag my attention away and look elsewhere.

We had come to the home of Mrs. Fisher with the express purpose of investigating a complaint we had heard that she had been mistreating her canine friend. But now it seemed clear that we'd arrived too late, for the person we were supposed to investigate under the guise of a visit from the Pet Owners Society was no longer with us.

Behind her sat the Bichon Frisé under consideration, and as we transferred our attention to the small white fluffy lapdog, it was clear that she wasn't taking too well to this sudden demise of her human.

"Bella, right?" asked Harriet, who was the first to recover from the shock of discovering our hostess dead. "My name is Harriet, and these are my friends Max, Dooley and Brutus."

Bella simply stared at us, clearly very impressed with these recent shocking events that had visited her home.

"Give her some space," Brutus advised. "She's obviously had a great shock and probably is in need of a little breathing room to process what happened."

"Oh, I know what happened," said the doggie, speaking up for the first time. "In fact, I know exactly what happened, and..." Suddenly she performed a sort of impromptu jig on the spot. "And I'm so happy! So happy I could sing! Sing my little heart out! The witch is dead—the witch is dead, yippee!"

I think it's safe to say we all stared at the small lapdog with horror written all over our features. It was no way to behave in the face of the tragedy that had just befallen the dog. And I think Dooley said it best when he stated, "It's the shock. It's made her go mad, the poor thing."

EXCERPT FROM PURRFECT ZOO (MAX 69)

"I'm not mad, I'm glad!" the doggie caroled happily. "This is the gladdest, happiest day of my whole life! The dragon has been slain, and I couldn't be happier!"

"Look, I'm all for the freedom of expression and all that," said Brutus, "but there are limits, Bella. Your human died, and you shouldn't celebrate. It's not done."

"Well, I'm doing it," said Bella. "And you can't stop me!" And to show us she wasn't kidding, she went skipping off in the direction of the house, singing a happy song all the while. And Brutus, as she had indicated, didn't stop her.

"Poor thing has gone completely crazy," said Harriet, shaking her head sadly.

"It's understandable," said Dooley. "If something were to happen to our humans, we would probably go a little crazy ourselves."

"Yeah, I guess so," said Brutus, who was staring after Bella as she passed through the pet flap and disappeared into the house. "But not so crazy we'd say a lot of very awful things about them. Calling the woman a witch. My God. After she probably starved herself so she could feed her dog. Maybe that's why she died, sacrificing herself for her precious pet."

"Maybe Bella wasn't all that fond of her human?" Dooley suggested finally, having given the matter some thought. "She did seem happy that she's dead."

But before we had a chance to go further into this peculiar example of the human-canine bond, Gran alerted us to the importance of keeping our wits about us and paying attention.

"I think she was murdered," our aged human now claimed. She had been taking a closer look at the dead woman and now straightened again.

"What makes you say that?" I asked.

"My main clue is the big butcher knife that's sticking out of her back."

## EXCERPT FROM PURRFECT ZOO (MAX 69)

We all moved to where Gran was pointing, and I saw she might just have a point. There was indeed a very large knife sticking out of the unfortunate Mrs. Chloe Fisher's back.

"That should do the trick," I agreed.

"Yeah, I don't think she put it there herself," Brutus indicated.

"Unless she fell from the swing and landed on top of the knife?" Dooley suggested, offering us an alternative view.

"She only fell off the swing after we arrived," Gran pointed out. "So she couldn't have fallen on that knife, Dooley. No, this woman was murdered, and if I'm not mistaken, it happened right before we arrived, so the murderer could still be in the area."

We all scanned the boxwood hedge that lined the backyard. Located behind the swing, it obscured the view of whatever was behind it, or whoever was hiding in there!

"You better take a look," Gran suggested, and for some reason, she was looking at Harriet and Brutus as she said it.

"Why us!" Harriet cried indignantly.

"Probably because we spend most of our time in the bushes," Brutus grunted, and with hanging paws, he and Harriet did as they were told and disappeared into that hedge. A couple of breathless moments later, they returned empty-pawed.

"No sign of any murderer in there," said Brutus. "There is a fence, though, so maybe he scaled it after having done the dirty deed and is now escaping via the neighboring gardens."

Gran decided that now that the coast was clear, she might as well take a gander herself, and so she headed for that fence and hoisted herself up to take a look at those neighboring gardens Brutus had mentioned.

"Nothing doing!" she announced after a moment. "I see a nice garden, a barbecue set, a pool, but no murderer."

She sounded relieved as she said it. It's one thing to come

## EXCERPT FROM PURRFECT ZOO (MAX 69)

upon a dead body, but another to come upon the person who made it so. The evil might not have expended itself yet, and the murderer just might turn his homicidal rage on the poor hapless witness!

Dooley must have followed the same line of thought, for he said, "I just hope he doesn't have more knives in his collection, Max." He shivered. "I don't think I would enjoy getting a knife planted in my back."

"No, I wouldn't either," I confessed.

Moments later, Gran was calling the police, and as she was relaying the facts of the case as they had presented themselves to us, I wondered where Mrs. Fisher's husband could be. The couple were supposed to meet us and talk to us together.

Gran must have asked herself the same question, for she now told the dispatcher, "And of the husband, there's no trace. So chances are that he's the killer." She listened for a moment. "Yeah, a big knife of the kitchen variety. The brand?" She glanced over at the hilt. "I'm sorry but I can't make out the brand since the knife has been shoved in all the way to the hilt. Yeah, all the way. Why?" She listened some more. "Yeah, I'm sure it must be a great quality knife, Dolores, nice and sharp. And I can understand how important it is for you to sample different brands for your big kitchen remodel that's coming up, but I'm not going to pull it out to check the brand on this one. You'll just have to ask the coroner when he gets here. Bye now."

She disconnected and shook her head. "I don't know if it's me, but Dolores seems to be going nuttier and nuttier."

"It's just you," Harriet assured her. "Dolores is a policewoman, so she's been dealing with murder all her life, making her jaded. We, on the other hand, are still pretty new at this, so we see it as a life-changing event, whereas to professionals like Dolores it's just one of those things."

It certainly seemed like a life-changing event to Chloe Fisher, I thought, as I overcame my natural aversion to dead people and studied the woman's body. Gran was right. That big knife would have done the trick. And as it had indeed been shoved in to the hilt, whoever the killer was must have used a lot of strength, for I didn't think it was easy to accomplish such a feat.

From the house, the sound of a doorbell sounded, and Gran shook her head. "I told Dolores the body was in the backyard, so why ring the front door?" But as she was heading for the house, suddenly a woman dressed in a red summer dress rounded the house, and when she saw us, hesitated for a moment before asking, "Is this Mike Fisher's house? It's just that I rang the bell but when no one answered I just figured..." She had now glanced behind us and saw the body, lying prone on the ground. The woman brought a distressed hand to her mouth and gasped in shock. "Is that... is she..."

"Dead," Gran confirmed. "No idea who made her that way, though. The police are on their way, so they should be here soon. Who are you, by the way?"

"Suzette," said the woman, still staring in horror and shock at the body. "Suzette Peters. I'm Mike's new colleague, and he told me to drop by so we could work on a project together."

"I haven't seen Mike, actually," said Gran, and now turned her attention to the house. "You don't think..." She glanced down at us, and I knew exactly what she was thinking.

"We're on it," I therefore announced and set paw for the house. We zipped through the pet flap Bella had disappeared through, and the four of us spread out to go in search of Mike, whose body just might be lying around somewhere, as dead as his wife. If Mike was supposed to be home, and Suzette's words seemed to confirm that, the killer might very

## EXCERPT FROM PURRFECT ZOO (MAX 69)

well have murdered both members of the household, or maybe even more if the Fishers had kids.

It was a contingency I found very hard to take into consideration, but then you sometimes hear these stories about entire families being murdered. But try as we might, we didn't see any sign of another presence in the house, whether dead or alive, except for Bella, of course, who was in the kitchen eating from her bowl and didn't seem to have a care in the world.

So after confirming to Gran that Mr. Fisher was absent from the premises, I returned to the kitchen and took a seat next to Bella. "So about your human," I said.

She looked up, a happy smile on her face. "Isn't this the gladdest day of all, Max? The most wonderful day? The sun is out, the witch is dead, and all is right with the world!"

"About that," I said, deciding to broach the topic gently, lest she suddenly snap out of whatever mood had taken her as a consequence of the shock of seeing her human being murdered in front of her own eyes, and attack me. "Did you see what happened just then? With the knife and the murderer and all?"

"Oh, no," she said immediately. "I know what you're doing, Max."

"You do? What am I doing?"

"You're trying to turn me into a witness to this crime. But I'm not going to do it. I'm not going to tell you who killed Chloe just so you can turn around and tell your human, who will tell the police, who will arrest the killer and put them in jail. No way. As far as I'm concerned, the killer did the world a great service, and should get a medal, not be punished with prison."

"You do realize that murdering people is generally frowned upon."

"I don't care. I laugh in the face of these artificial societal constructs, Max. I laugh in the face of justice being done. And I laugh at Chloe's killer and thank them, for they rescued me from a life of constant strife and turmoil."

"Chloe wasn't a nice person?" I ventured.

"Nice!" she scoffed. "She was horrible! Always shouting at me, and sometimes she would even pinch me, Max. Pinch me hard!"

"But why would she pinch you?"

"No reason at all! Just because she liked it! She was cruel, Max. Very cruel. And cruelest of all to Mike and to their daughter Allison, who could never do anything right."

"Did she pinch them also?"

"Oh, she did worse than that. She destroyed them with her tongue."

Dooley, who had joined us, now frowned. "How do you destroy someone with your tongue, Bella? Unless she had a very long tongue that could lash out like a whip?"

"Words, Dooley," said Bella. "She destroyed people with words. She wasn't just physically violent, but she was also mean and cruel and could say the most horrible things."

"Okay, so where is Mike?" I asked. "And where is Allison?"

She gave me a keen look. "Now, wouldn't you like to know that?"

"Yeah, I would like to know that," I confirmed. "Because if what you're saying is true, then either Mike or Allison or both have just graduated to the position of prime suspect."

But if I had hoped this would cause Bella to give us a clue as to the whereabouts of Mike or Allison and whether either of them was Chloe's murderer, she wasn't giving an inch. "No way am I helping you guys capture Chloe's killer. Unless you want to give the person a medal."

"We could give them a medal," I said, "for the best arts and crafts made in prison."

She smiled a sly smile. "I think you'll find that you won't

## EXCERPT FROM PURRFECT ZOO (MAX 69)

be able to break me, Max. I've been at the receiving end of so much verbal abuse that your words can't hurt me."

"I have no intention whatsoever of hurting you, Bella. But in polite society, murder is generally discouraged, and whoever perpetrates it is typically punished, otherwise everyone would start murdering each other with impunity. And we can't have that, now can we?"

"Oh, yes, we can," she said. "If the victim deserves to be murdered I think it's fine."

I decided that my attempts to get a witness statement out of her were in vain and decided to leave it for now. Dooley wasn't giving up so easily, though. "You can't really defend a murderer, Bella," he said. "Murder is wrong!"

"A social construct that I think you'll find isn't always appropriate," she said, causing Dooley to goggle at her to some extent.

"But, but, but..."

"I know it's unusual to side with the murderer of one's own human," said Bella, "but in this case, I can assure you it's the only correct position to take, Dooley. And now if you'll excuse me, I have to head to the dog park to tell my friends the good news!"

And with these words, she was off, leaving us dumbfounded, flabbergasted, and even nonplussed!

## ABOUT NIC

Nic has a background in political science and before being struck by the writing bug worked odd jobs around the world (including but not limited to massage therapist in Mexico, gardener in Italy, restaurant manager in India, and Berlitz teacher in Belgium).

When he's not writing he enjoys curling up with a good (comic) book, watching British crime dramas, French comedies or Nancy Meyers movies, sampling pastry (apple cake!), pasta and chocolate (preferably the dark variety), twisting himself into a pretzel doing morning yoga, going for a run, and spoiling his big red tomcat Tommy.

He lives with his wife (and aforementioned cat) in a small village smack dab in the middle of absolutely nowhere and is probably writing his next 'Mysteries of Max' book right now.

www.nicsaint.com

## ALSO BY NIC SAINT

**The Mysteries of Max**
Purrfect Murder
Purrfectly Deadly
Purrfect Revenge
Purrfect Heat
Purrfect Crime
Purrfect Rivalry
Purrfect Peril
Purrfect Secret
Purrfect Alibi
Purrfect Obsession
Purrfect Betrayal
Purrfectly Clueless
Purrfectly Royal
Purrfect Cut
Purrfect Trap
Purrfectly Hidden
Purrfect Kill
Purrfect Boy Toy
Purrfectly Dogged
Purrfectly Dead
Purrfect Saint
Purrfect Advice
Purrfect Passion

A Purrfect Gnomeful

Purrfect Cover

Purrfect Patsy

Purrfect Son

Purrfect Fool

Purrfect Fitness

Purrfect Setup

Purrfect Sidekick

Purrfect Deceit

Purrfect Ruse

Purrfect Swing

Purrfect Cruise

Purrfect Harmony

Purrfect Sparkle

Purrfect Cure

Purrfect Cheat

Purrfect Catch

Purrfect Design

Purrfect Life

Purrfect Thief

Purrfect Crust

Purrfect Bachelor

Purrfect Double

Purrfect Date

Purrfect Hit

Purrfect Baby

Purrfect Mess

Purrfect Paris

Purrfect Model
Purrfect Slug
Purrfect Match
Purrfect Game
Purrfect Bouquet
Purrfect Home
Purrfectly Slim
Purrfect Nap
Purrfect Yacht
Purrfect Scam
Purrfect Fury
Purrfect Christmas
Purrfect Gems
Purrfect Demons
Purrfect Show
Purrfect Impasse
Purrfect Charade

**The Mysteries of Max Collections**

Collection 1 (Books 1-3)
Collection 2 (Books 4-6)
Collection 3 (Books 7-9)
Collection 4 (Books 10-12)
Collection 5 (Books 13-15)
Collection 6 (Books 16-18)
Collection 7 (Books 19-21)
Collection 8 (Books 22-24)
Collection 9 (Books 25-27)
Collection 10 (Books 28-30)

Collection 11 (Books 31-33)
Collection 12 (Books 34-36)
Collection 13 (Books 37-39)
Collection 14 (Books 40-42)
Collection 15 (Books 43-45)
Collection 16 (Books 46-48)
Collection 17 (Books 49-51)
Collection 18 (Books 52-54)
Collection 19 (Books 55-57)
Collection 20 (Books 58-60)
Collection 21 (Books 61-63)
Collection 22 (Books 64-66)

## The Mysteries of Max Big Collections

Big Collection 1 (Books 1-10)
Big Collection 2 (Books 11-20)

## The Mysteries of Max Short Stories

Collection 1 (Stories 1-3)
Collection 2 (Stories 4-7)

### Nora Steel

Murder Retreat

### The Kellys

Murder Motel
Death in Suburbia

### Emily Stone

Murder at the Art Class

**Washington & Jefferson**

First Shot

**Alice Whitehouse**

Spooky Times

Spooky Trills

Spooky End

Spooky Spells

**Ghosts of London**

Between a Ghost and a Spooky Place

Public Ghost Number One

Ghost Save the Queen

Box Set 1 (Books 1-3)

A Tale of Two Harrys

Ghost of Girlband Past

Ghostlier Things

**Charleneland**

Deadly Ride

Final Ride

**Neighborhood Witch Committee**

Witchy Start

Witchy Worries

Witchy Wishes

**Saffron Diffley**

Crime and Retribution

Vice and Verdict

Felonies and Penalties (Saffron Diffley Short 1)

**The B-Team**

Once Upon a Spy

**Tate-à-Tate**

Enemy of the Tates

**Ghosts vs. Spies**

The Ghost Who Came in from the Cold

**Witchy Fingers**

Witchy Trouble

Witchy Hexations

Witchy Possessions

Witchy Riches

Box Set 1 (Books 1-4)

**The Mysteries of Bell & Whitehouse**

One Spoonful of Trouble

Two Scoops of Murder

Three Shots of Disaster

Box Set 1 (Books 1-3)

A Twist of Wraith

A Touch of Ghost

A Clash of Spooks

Box Set 2 (Books 4-6)

The Stuffing of Nightmares

A Breath of Dead Air

An Act of Hodd

Box Set 3 (Books 7-9)

A Game of Dons

**Standalone Novels**

When in Bruges

The Whiskered Spy

**ThrillFix**

Homejacking

The Eighth Billionaire

The Wrong Woman

Made in the USA
Las Vegas, NV
02 December 2023